JULIE LANDSMAN
2801 43RD AVE. S.
MINNEAPOLIS, MN 55406

LAST SUMMER

LAST SUMMER
Stories by Davida Kilgore

Minnesota Voices Project Number 34

NEW RIVERS PRESS 1988

Copyright © 1988 by Davida Kilgore
Library of Congress Catalog Card Number: 88-60054
ISBN 0-89823-103-5
All rights reserved
Typesetting: Peregrine Publications
Author photo by Anthony Vulney Hall
Graphics by Seitu Jones

The story "Bingo" appeared in *Stiller's Pond: New Fiction from the Upper Midwest* (New Rivers Press, 1988).

The author wishes to thank Susan Welch for his invaluable editorial assitance.

Last Summer has been published with the aid of grants from the Jerome Foundation, the First Bank System Foundation, the United Arts Council (with funds provided in part by the McKnight Foundation), and the National Endowment for the Arts (with funds appropriated by the Congress of the United States).

New Rivers Press books are distributed by

The Talman Company	and	Bookslinger
150 - 5th Avenue		213 East 4th Street
New York, NY 10011		St. Paul, MN 55101

Last Summer has been manufactured in the United States of America for New Rivers Press, Inc. (C. W. Truesdale, editor/publisher), 1602 Selby Avenue, St. Paul, MN 55104 in a first edition of 1,500 copies.

After years of fighting over the virtues of law school, three weeks before my Mama died she bought me a typewriter and told me to go for it. And so Last Summer and Other Stories *is lovingly dedicated to my Mama.*

Della Delora Kilgore

CONTENTS

- 1   Bingo
- 19   The Day We Discovered We Were Black
- 27   Unpaid Debts
- 39   Three Alarm Fire
- 47   The Dietary Exploits of Bessie (A Fable)
- 57   Last Summer
- 71   Heaven Vs. Hell
- 83   The Deterioration of 47th Street (an excerpt)

Bingo

It was all a bad mistake. I shoulda knowed something was gonna go wrong cause the bingo game at the VFW Hall was ten minutes late starting and Harry Wade don't never be late in taking our money. But it was 1:40 in the afternoon when that little piece of man hunched up them stairs on the side of the 'lectric numbers board, perched on his bar stool, and pretended to smile at us, ying-yanging that spiel we all knows by heart. Old Harry's got a megaphone voice, but he always uses the mike anyways, trying to amplify hisself into something he ain't; looking down on us from that platform like Pharaoh gotta hold of Moses and made him promise to lead us to the land of bankruptcy. Not too many peoples like Harry, and he don't like too many peoples, either, but he loves our money and we love to play bingo, and when you play with the devil . . . Harry kept on flapping his jaws while we did our last minute card switching, ordered sandwiches and pop, and got our hands stamped.

"Good afternoon, all you nice ladies and gentlemen. Welcome to another Wednesday afternoon of bingo. As all you good people know, our Wednesday afternoon session is sponsored by the Sacred Order of the Purple Heart."

I like playing bingo, specially on Wednesdays, since even with my short legs, the VFW is stepping distance from my doctor's office . . . no matter what that man says about my blood pressure. That's all he ever says — "Jean Thompson, you have to take it easy. There's no need in taking the risk of getting yourself all worked up." — I tells him, "Hon, at 65, getting up in the morning is risky. And don't nothing much happen at the bingo hall to get excited about; you either win or you don't." After all, I ain't no big time Al Capone gambler like my best friend, Marie Jenkins. But I do enjoy playing me a little bit on Wednesdays, Thursdays, and sometimes Sunday nights, even if it do mean putting up with the likes of Harry.

Harry went on with his speech. "Now all you fine people know that we play the big games here on Wednesday afternoons: $50, $75, $100 Progressives, Gambler's Choice, chance at a black-and-white TV or $50 cash, and of course, the Fishbowl. Our first half-hour we'll be playing Free Card games. A single winner bingoing on the last number called will play however many sets he or she is playing free all afternoon, including the big games. All unplayed cards must be face down and there will be no switching of cards after the first number is called.

"Cards are 3 for a dime, 10 for 30, 14 for 40, 18 for 50 and so on, up to ten sets. For your dining pleasure, the girls will be serving hot and cold sandwiches, pop and the best quarter cup of coffee money can buy."

Marie and I checked our cards one last time while Harry finished up his speech. We always got to the Hall by at least 12:45 to choose her cards. We had to. Marie had her own private system and you just don't know how hard it is to shift through umpteen cards, stacked fifty and sixty deep, trying to find her favorite combinations. See, I don't study up on bingo like Marie, to me a card is a card. I just pick em up and throw em down on the table. And couldn't care less what color they are. But not only did Marie have to play her favorite numbers, all the cards had to have red borders to boot. You just try finding a red 1/2 corner combination sometimes when you ain't got nothing better to do.

But Marie always said, "Jean, there are some cards you have to have or you may as well stay your ass at home. You have to have a 3/13, 65/75, and a 61/71 in the corners. You have to have at least one Straight-10, 20, 60, 70, and if you're going to play Ns, get yourself a 33/43, 31/41, and that damn 37 always goes with that damn 39."

Child, I know it sounds silly going through all these motions to pick some cards cause you could pick till your fingers fell off and Harry'd still call whatever number you didn't need. But I enjoyed Marie's company and quiet as it's kept, I was partial to a 62/72 combination myself. Besides, Marie had been playing bingo seven days a week, two sessions a day for the past ten years, and if she didn't know what she was doing, who would?

Harry clicked on the machine and the balls commenced to bouncing offa each other like kernels turning theyselves into popcorn in the big popper near the entrance door at KMART. Marie knew the colors of those balls by heart. She would say, "If Harry would just shut-up for a minute, I could look my number out." Harry said, "Our first number out will be the Fishbowl number. Every time we call this number, we'll add five dollars to this little fishbowl on the counter, and some time after four o'clock we'll play a special game for all the money inside it.

"We're ready to start our Free-Card games. Anything goes: Straights, Corners, Angles, Postage Stamps, Inside/Outside Diamonds, Inside/Outside Squares – they're all good. Good luck, now! Your first, and Fishbowl number is . . . 0 . . . 75."

Marie mugged her lucky grin cause she always played herself some 0/75s. See, that number had been a winner for her . . . about . . . umm? . . . three years ago and she said, "You don't change a good thing. That number's hot and all I have to do is wait – it'll be hot again. You wait and see." And Lawd knows we'd been waiting – for months now. But that was Marie; she had more patience than a little bit, would put up with shit I wouldn't think about taking.

Everybody at the Wednesday afternoon – or any afternoon or evening session for that matter – knew Marie Jenkins. Yes, Lawd, Marie was one good-lookin woman for "sixty years young," as she used to tell it. You couldn't miss her: 200-some-odd pounds squeezed into them old-fashioned red stretch pants with the seams down the front, a matching red imitation silk blouse, and red patent leather, open-toed pumps. We all knew that Wednesday was her lucky day and red was her favorite color. We knew everything about Marie, or so we thought, cluding the fact that along with the red magnetic bingo chips with the matching magnetic wand to swoop them up with, Marie had a .38 inside that big old purse of hers.

Marie drove a five-year-old New Yorker that she kept in better shape than herself, or her house, which was the excuse her husband Fred, that old Poindexter-looking chippy, used to justify his affair with this here chick name of Thelma.

Thelma's one of those 35 year old heifers don't have the sense to realize she ain't a teenager no more. She wears those skin-tight shimmy britches and low-cut sweaters; bras so small they make her look like she's got three instead of two. The kind of woman, and I'm using the term loosely, that old men get off on. And since she always sat four rows across from us at the Hall, Marie had to put up with Thelma's laughing and pointing at her all during the session.

Marie was just as sweet as she could be and that's why all of us, well all of us 'cepting Harry, and Thelma and her crowd, just loved her to death. Marie remembered birthdays when our own children didn't; she visited the sick and shut-ins listed in the church bulletin; if she had a dollar, you had fifty cents if you needed it; no one who knew her ever went hungry. And because we knew she'd do the same for us, we suffered right alongside her through her children's divorces, her colds, flus and recent operation. And Fred's death.

I'd almost forgotten Fred'd been gone one year to the day till I looked at Marie and saw the way she was staring at Thelma. If looks could kill, Thelma'd be dead. I felt like maybe I should say something but Marie beat me to it: "Know why I was late getting here? I went out to the cemetery to put some fresh flowers on Fred's grave. It surprised me that I still miss him considering what he did to me. And to have to come up here and look at Thelma. I've already had one run-in with her today . . . Thank God we had those pre-paid burial plots."

I didn't find out till after the funeral that things had been bad for Marie for a long time. She always did so much for everybody else I figgered she was sitting high on the hog. Turns out Fred hadn't been paying the bills, or his insurance premiums, spending all his money on Thelma, instead, and Marie had been playing catch-up for months.

Why just this morning she'd shivered in a two-block long

government-hand-out line, waiting to get the cheese and butter Thelma and her friends volunteered to pass out every third Wednesday of the month. And Marie was so proud that I wouldn't've even known she'd been to the community center for help if that scandalous hussy, Thelma, hadn't blabbed it all over the Hall.

I swear Thelma ain't nothing but an old refrigerator, can't keep nothing. You should've heard the things she was saying about Marie before she got to the hall today. Just couldn't wait to tell it: "You should have seen the old bingo queen. She was crying and begging us for some food, trying to con us into paying her NSP bill. I told her, 'If you'd stop playing so damn much bingo, you could keep your lights on.' I told her, 'We only help people with a real emergency and if you have enough money to play bingo, then you'd have enough money to pay your bills.' I told her – "

Nobody really gave a damn what else Thelma told Marie cause we all knowed it was Thelma, herself, who had spread the word about her and Fred in the first place. I knowed about that tramp and people's husbands from the git-go, but I would never have told Marie; some things better to find out for yourself. So it was bad enough Marie needed to win big today, but having to deal with Thelma sitting four rows away, gossiping to anyone who would listen, was a little much. I hoped Marie would win the Coverall and then tell Thelma to go kiss her own ass.

And Marie would tell her, too. She sang tenor in the church choir every Sunday morning, and yelled "Bingo" in bass every Sunday afternoon from the third chair from the right, third row from the right wall of the Hall. She was a God-fearing woman but let's face it, bingo brings out the worst in a person.

Take Marie again. Marie didn't like Harry, called him everything the rest of us felt about him but didn't quite have the nerve to say – in public, anyways. Her favorite line, the one she used when Harry didn't call her out was, "You old bald-headed, skinny-assed white bastard! Why don't you shake up your balls?"

Harry, he would cheese at her and say, "Why don't you come up here shake them for me – heh, heh."

Marie would give him this po'-fool look, say, "Don't you wish?" and then the two of them would cut loose. They ignored the big "NO CURSING OR SWEARING ALLOWED" sign near the exit door and played them some dozens. But Harry ain't no complete fool. He wouldn't dare try and throw Marie outta the Hall.

Well, like I was saying, Harry called out 0/75 and Marie covered her numbers.

"B-10! I-19!"

Marie popped me on my arm and pointed at her cards. She had an out for a G.

"Jean," she said, "that old fart gave me my out. All he has to do is call any G: 46, 50, 60, any of the good ones, and I don't give a damn which one it is." Then she yelled up at Harry, "Be nice!" and I noticed her hand was shaking as Harry turned the purple ball in his hand. Purple balls are Gs.

"G-60!"

"Bingo!" Marie's voice bounced offa the walls – and our ear drums. Thelma and her crowd muttered, "Shit, that old broad always plays free." They knew that was a lie. It had been a long time since Marie had won the Free-Card game. The rest of us yelled, "Go get him, Marie."

One of the collectors, name of Lucy, jogged over to our table and snatched Marie's card, knocking her chips across the table; some of them even rolled on the floor. Lucy called out, "Straight-10, 19, 60, 75."

Harry didn't like it worth shit. He hated it when Marie won to play free all day but he said, "One good bingo stopping on G-60. Are there are other bingos?"

He knew there weren't.

"Ten sets?"

Lucy nodded. Harry knew Marie always played ten sets.

"Ten sets free all afternoon to that lucky player."

Lucy brought over a five-by-seven, ten of spades playing card in a lucite picture frame that stood for Marie's ten free sets, slammed in on the table and I could just hear her thinking to herself, "I can't short change her today, but there's always that old biddy at the other end of my station, she never counts her change." One of these days someone is going to count their change and knock that cheap blonde wig off Lucy's head.

For the next twenty-eight minutes Marie made sure her cards had all the numbers Harry was calling. Her 61/71 combination was called. She changed a couple of other cards, between games like you're supposed to. I played a game for her while she went to the bathroom and by the time she came back to her seat, Harry was announcing the $100 Progressive.

"Okay, folks, it's time for our first big game of the afternoon. Cards in this game are ten cents apiece, no bonus cards. Straight bingo in five numbers or less for 100 dollars! Just a reminder, folks: We know our Wednesday afternoon crowd is always honest . . . "

Somebody in the back of the Hall laughed. I can't prove it but I think that that part of Harry's speech is a signal to one of his house-players, and the collectors, that he didn't want any of the regular customers to win this game. Like I said, I can't prove it but it seems like one of the house-players wins every time Harry gives that speech.

"There will be no switching of cards after the first number is called. And remember, the last number called must be used in your bingo to have it honored. All unplayed cards face down. Everybody ready?"

Somebody yelled, "Shake your balls."

Harry, he said, "I'm too old to be shaking my balls . . . heh, heh, heh."

"I know that's right," Marie yelled back. Harry rolled his eyes at her and called the first number.

"Your first number out is 0 . . . 75."

Everybody yelled, "Fishbowl!"

"We'll add five dollars to the Fishbowl. Next number out: N-39. B/13 . . . I/20 . . . B/8 . . ."

Peoples started screaming at Harry:

"Slow down, fool."

"Where's the fire?"

"I'm still on B/13."

"Call the next number, will ya?"

Harry gave us a little time to catch up. "Okay, we'll slow it down. B/8 was your fifth number. Continuing on, we're looking for any bingo with the calling of N/37."

Marie covered her N/37s, realized she had an out, popped me on the arm again, and said, "G/51 will give me an inside diamond, and he hasn't called a G yet. Everybody's waiting on one, but a split is still money."

Marie didn't think bout an I being called would give somebody a Postage Stamp cause she didn't have an I out. Harry grabbed a green ball, called out, "I/23," and an elderly man, sitting way back yonder in the no-smoking section yelled, "Bingo!"

"Bingo," screamed the collector as she jogged over to the man's table and picked up his card. Harry shut down the machine. "Bingo has been called; hold your cards, please."

The collector called out, "Stamp-8, 13, 20, 23."

"That's a good bingo," Harry said, "using I/23. Pay that lucky winner $50."

Naturally, Marie thought it was unfair. She started bitching: "That old coot's only playing three cards and he wins $50. Harry could have called a G if he'd wanted to, damn his time. Always freaking with somebody's out."

"Come on, Marie," I said, patting her hand. "It's just the first big game and you're playing free, so you ain't losing nothing. You still got all afternoon to win."

I'm usually pretty good at calming her down, so when Lucy came around to collect for the next game, I ordered two coffees: one with extra cream and sugar for Marie. She spilled coffee, chain smoked Kools and started up, again.

"Why doesn't he play Crazy? Hell, I always win something with Crazy bingo. Why doesn't he play Three-Corners? Those are the only damn outs he's been giving me. Now you watch, he'll play Three-Corners and then he'll only give me two."

I didn't waste my breath arguing with her. Marie knew Harry never played Crazy or Three-Cornered bingo on Wednesdays. She knew that, usually, if you was playing free all day, you didn't win any money. Like the rich folks say, you got to spend money to make money. Some peoples lucked out and broke the free-playing jinx, and like somebody else say, rules were made to be broken. Well, if that was true, Marie needed to break one today cause NSP has rules, too, and the hardest one to get around is the due date on the fifteenth of the month, so rule on that.

That damn 0/75 must have come up every other game. Seems like to me we was hollering "Fishbowl" so often there had to be at least $65 in the pot. Marie kept punching me on my arm.

"Just let me need that damn 75. Harry'll call 70, 71, 72, 3 or 4. I could smack his ass off of that stool."

"Shake up your balls, " screamed a halter-topped redhead with saggy breasts.

Harry, he said, "Come shake them for me, cutie," and liked to slobber all over hisself about that girl. Then he jumped off his stool, turned off the machine, and pretended to mix up the balls. And let me tell you something: I bet if that broad gives Harry a little play, she'll be a house-player in no time flat.

Cause Harry's so trifling. Sometimes, not too often mind you, but sometimes I felt kinda sorry for him. Those big bingo parlors on the Indian reservations were damn near driving him outta business. Them places had $10,000 and $100,000 pay-offs an those big money pull-tabs. Nickel-and-dime joints like Harry's weren't as packed as they used to be and he still had to pay rent and utilities. Lucy and her gang were ripping him off; rumor had it the house-players wanted a bigger cut of the action to keep coming. But Harry was so scantchy I couldn't feel too sorry for him. He cheated us, his employees cheated him, and like Marie always said: "God don't like ugly."

At three o'clock we played another big game. The Hall was getting crowded so Harry did his thing, again.

"Okay, folks, it's time for our second big game of the day . . ." He went blah, blah, blah, same old speech, and had the nerve to ask, "Everybody ready?"

"We've been ready for five minutes now. Just call, will ya. Jackass!"

"Shake up your balls!"

"Same winners all the time!"

Harry grinned. We all knew who the house-players were, and Harry knew we knew.

That thug Frank, with his slicker than slick self, could walk into the Hall just as a game was starting, throw down ten sets of cards, Helen would slither past him without collecting a dime, and Frank would win — just like that.

It's not like them big bingo parlors where they held your card in front of another player's face so somebody could see the bingo was legit. At these small halls the collector just picked up your card and started reading it back in front of her own face. Helen could make up any numbers she wanted to and from the catch in her voice and sneaky peeks at the board, I knew good and damn well that was exactly what she did. But how you gonna prove it?

Harry started calling. "N/31 is the first number out."

Marie covered her N/31s. I heard her pray: "Come on, Lord. You know I need this win. Pleasepleaseplease, just this one time and I swear I won't come here no more."

"N/41. N/35."

"Slow down please, Harry," said Thelma.

I don't know who Thelma thought she was fooling but I knew when she said that she was up to her old tricks again. What usually happens is one of her crew sits out a game and searches through the unplayed cards on her table, looking for a card with most of the numbers on it that Harry's calling. It don't have to have all the numbers, just close enough in case anyone happens to get a quick glance at it. Then she'll slip Thelma the card under the table, Thelma'll call "Bingo" and the two of them split the money, minus Harry's cut, of course, Marie popped me on the arm and nodded in Thelma's direction cause she was as hip to that game as I was.

Peoples was still yelling at Harry. "Same numbers you called the last game." Frank, with his cheating ass, had to make it look good.

"G/52."

I could see Marie's shoulders tighten. Four numbers called, two to go, and all she needed was one more N. She smacked me, pointed at her cards, and yelled, "Come on, you old fool, call my N, damn it."

"O/75!"

"Fishbowl!"

Harry announced, "Seventy-five dollars in the fishbowl, folks."

"Damn the Fishbowl," Marie yelled. "Call my N. Been needing a N since the third number."

Marie started sweating and grinding her teeth. I knows how she felt. You'd get those three numbered outs and then you'd wait . . . and wait . . . and wait, and Harry never did call your number. I knew Harry wouldn't call another N. So did Marie.

The sixth number was B/2 and Marie looked like she wanted to cry. "Three damn chances and he calls a B. Well, at least let me win the fifty. Call my N right now."

Harry said, "B/2 was your sixth number. It's now an anything goes game with the calling of I/17."

I didn't need the $50 as much as Marie did, but I'd already lost twenty and $50 is $50. I never say what number I be waiting on cause that's bad luck, so Marie didn't know I need I/17. And much as I loved her, I enjoyed yelling "Bingo."

Lucy grabbed my card, flashed her teeth at Marie, and called back my numbers. Harry honored it: "One good bingo using I/17. Pay that lucky winner $50. Congratulations, Jean."

Marie and I watched as Lucy counted out three tens, two fives, ten ones and laid them on my table. Her wig shifted as she threw her head and switched back to the waitress station to record the payoff. I started to ask Marie if she wanted to borrow a few dollars, and she looked like she wanted to ask for a loan, but didn't neither one of us say nothing. Harry started calling the next game.

"N/45."

That was the N Marie needed for the fifty dollars. Harry knew it, Lucy knew it, the regulars knew it. We all knew Marie played a red card with Ns-31, 41, 35, 45, and held our breaths expecting her to go off and call Harry everything but a child of God. But Marie didn't say a word. Not one damn word.

Harry wasn't even trying to stop hisself from laughing. I can't prove it, but I've always been under the impression that he wore those ugly, long-sleeved flannel shirts so he could slip a ball up his sleeve in case he didn't get a signal from one of the house-players. Harry hated to give up $100 till the last of the big games and he wasn't too happy about giving it up then, specially since the Wednesday Coverall was $500. And he really didn't want Marie to win the hundred after Thelma tipped him off about Marie's NSP bill. Harry hated Marie enough to make sure she didn't win a dime. If she did win anything big, there'd be a trick in it.

By now the Hall was cigarette-smoke foggy; bingo halls about the only place left smokers got any say-so. Harry be bitching about how much it cost to run the air-conditioner on high, but he couldn't breathe no better than the rest of us so he turned it up. Once that air kicked in, it didn't take long to get chilly. Peoples draped sweaters across they shoulders but Marie was sweating across her forehead and down her neck; she had loosed the top of her blouse and her eyes looked glazed. Didn't look too good to me, but Marie kept covering numbers as Harry said, "B/11 . . . B/3 . . . B/13."

That 3/13 combination was another one of Marie's favorites and I offered up a silent prayer, "Please Lawd, let her win something." I asked Marie if she wanted a Coke. She shook her head, "No."

"I/24 . . . G/56."

All Marie needed was 0/72 and I knew she would perk up, so I left her alone. Harry had a red ball in his hand — an 0.

"0/72!"

Sounded like everybody and they momma yelled, "Bingo." Marie never opened her mouth. She just sat there while Harry said each collector's name as she called back numbers.

"Marge?"

Marge read Thelma's card; Harry honored it. Dawn read Mattie Sampson's card; Harry honored it. There were too many winners to count; Harry kept on honoring. Marie still hadn't claimed her bingo so I called Lucy over to get the cards. I knowed Marie had three winners cause she always took them cards home with her after the game. Then I took me an extra hard look at Marie cause it weren't like her to sleep a bingo.

"Got another bingo, Jean?"

"No, but Marie's got three."

"I didn't hear her yell anything."

Lucy and me was talking about Marie like she weren't sitting right there. I thought she would snap out of it when Lucy said, "Next time call your own bingo" cause Marie never let Lucy have the last say about nothing. But she just listened as Lucy called out:

"Harry, here's some more: 3, 24, 56, 72 . . . 13, 24, 56, 72 — twice."

"That's good. Any more? Okay, folks, we've got a bunch of winners; pay each two bucks."

Lucy threw four crumpled and two Scotch-taped dollar bills down on the table. Marie never picked up the money, just flicked Lucy a look. And there was something else in her face, too. Something like death warming up. Thought it was maybe leftovers from her surgery. I told Marie she'd come out of the house too soon, told her she should have stayed home at least a month. Told her the same thing the summer she had that operation and had to play bingo sitting on one of those plastic donuts.

I figgered Marie was simply worn out. Bingo could play hell with your nerves, specially when you really needed to win. You'd get good outs, and like I said, after waiting and waiting and waiting for your ship to come in, it upped and did a Titanic on your ass; bes that way, sometimes. But there was only one game left before the Coverall and then Marie could go home and get righteous before the evening session. I'd never known her not to bounce back. And I knowed for a fact that Harry, Lucy and Thelma — for all her big talk bout Marie, Thelma played as much bingo as anybody — would catch hell at the evening session.

"Well, folks," said Harry, "following our Fishbowl game, we'll be playing the Coverall. The Coverall today is $500 in fifty-six numbers or less. After the fifty-sixth number the pay-out is $250.

"But first, we have $125 in the Fishbowl. Anything goes and we'll play it until we get a single winner. Cards are ten cents each. All unplayed cards face down. Your first number out is G . . . 48."

The Fishbowl game wasn't nothing but a money-maker for the Hall. We replayed it five times before Tim, a collector who played on his days off, hit by hisself. Dawn called back his card and Harry said, "That's good! Pay that lucky winner $125." Hell yes it was good — for Harry — cause we all knew Tim had to kick-back fifty bucks.

"The Coverall is our last game of the Wednesday afternoon session. We'll give you a little time to change your cards, and we'll give these balls a big shake."

Harry hopped up and swiveled his hips like he thought he was some dead-and-gone Elvis Presley. Some of the new players laughed, but the rest of us just shook our heads knowing ain't no fool like an old fool. Harry was just killing time, waiting for the latecomers to get situated. At least they had enough sense to hold out till the last minute and only blow a dime a card rather than sitting there all afternoon going broke. After all, you only needed one card to win and just last week Cassandra Martin had walked in, spent the last thirty cents she had to her name — and I knowed it was her last cause her old man had just walked out on her and them four little babies — and hit the Coverall. So see there, God do answer prayer. I just hoped He was listening to Marie.

It had gotten awfully quiet in the Hall. Couldn't quite put my finger on it at first, but then it dawned on me: Marie wasn't cussing anybody out. She usually cut up right before the Coverall, saying things like:

"Shake up those balls, Harry! Hey, Lucy, tell that chick to get off her lazy ass and bring me a Coke with a lot of ice. You better not start calling yet. I haven't been to the john in two hours."

We'd crack up as Marie made a bee-line to the ladies' room. As soon as Harry heard the toilet flush, he'd call the first number. Marie'd sashay through the door, hitching in her get-along, still shaking her hands dry, ball up a fist at him and yell, "One of these days I'm going to catch you in the parking lot and then you better give your heart to God because your ass is going to belong to me."

Harry'd dare her, "You want to repeat that?" and Marie'd pat the side of her purse and say, "I didn't stutter! I can show you better than I can tell you." Harry suspected Marie was just selling wolf tickets, but he weren't taking no chances on the price of admission just in case she wasn't. He knew about that .38 as well as the rest of us did and like I said, Harry wasn't no complete fool. He didn't call another number till Marie was in her seat.

Marie didn't say nothing today but, "I'm glad it's time for the Coverall; it's too damn hot in here. Why doesn't Harry turn up the air-conditioner, clear out all this smoke. After I win this $500 I'll run down to NSP, have those bastards turn my lights back on and then go home and slip out of this headache so I'll be ready to play tonight."

I looked at Marie . . . and Lawd have mercy, sweat was still sliding down her face. I hoped she wasn't too upset over that $50 I'd won but I didn't think she was. Marie wasn't like that, not with her friends, anyways. Now if Thelma had hit for more than those two dollars, well, that would have been a different story.

All of a sudden I started feeling guilty cause in a way, I weren't behaving no better than Thelma. Don't know what I'd been thinking about before but I decided right then and there if Marie didn't win the Coverall I would have her over for dinner and write out a check so she could get her lights back on. I couldn't just let her sit in the dark. Ain't loaded or nothing like that but if I cut out bingo for a week – I could go that long with no problem, catch up on my housework – it wouldn't be no skin off my nose to give her the money and I knowed Marie would do the same for me.

Marie finally picked her win up off the table and stuffed them raggedy little bills in her purse. Instead of putting the purse back on the floor, she left it in her lap and I could see the butt of her .38. I said, "Marie, it's against the law to carry a concealed weapon. I don't care if Fred did give it to you for protection. You're gonna get in boocoo trouble with that thing one of these days."

"Jean, Fred said if I'm going to walk around with a purse full of money from playing bingo, and everybody knew it, that I needed something in case of an emergency. That's why I let everybody know I have it. I'd blow their damn heads off, trying to rob me. You see I've never been robbed, don't you?"

She had a point, but I still didn't like her carrying a gun around, and a loaded one at that. You hear all the time about how somebody blowed their head off accidentally.

"Who are you going to scare with an unloaded gun?"

"This is true," I said, "but still . . . one of these days." I let it drop as Harry started the Coverall.

"Everybody ready? The first number out is B/1."

By the sixteenth number, all you could hear were peoples shouting: "Slow down, fool!"

"That number ain't been out all day. He must've let it slip outta his sleeve."

"I've got a board don't have no numbers on it yet."

Marie covered her numbers, smiling to herself. Five or six of her boards were filling up pretty good and I figgered she was remembering a story she told me a few months ago. I wasn't sure if it was true or not, but knowing Marie, it probably was. The story went like this:

"Jean, Harry slipped up and let me win the Coverall. And you know how they pay you in those new, crisp, hundred dollar bills? Well, Lucy was too lazy to snap them apart like she usually does and I got me an extra hundred. Did I give it back? Hell no, I didn't give it back. Lucy's always short changing folks, and I would've loved to see her trying to explain to Harry why her station was $100 off. She didn't work here for a couple of months after that, remember?"

I laughed when Marie told me about it, although I was tempted to remind her that God don't like ugly. But it was good to see somebody getting that old buzzard back for a change – him and Lucy.

Harry kept on calling numbers:

"B/15 . . . N/32 . . . N/41 . . . G/60 . . . B/10 . . . O . . ."

"Oh, slow down," shouted somebody from the back of the Hall.

"Oh, okay," said Harry. "O/70 is your next number."

The fiftieth number was G/48. Marie popped me on my arm. She had an out for the Fishbowl number: O/75. That number had been called all day but it hadn't showed up yet in the Coverall. The fifty-first number was N/39.

"I/18 . . . I/16 . . G/57."

Word spread around the Hall that Marie needed 0/75. I'd told her about letting peoples know what number you need. She didn't know it but most of us were paying more attention to her than we was to our own cards.

Harry grabbed a red ball, an 0. Marie covered her 75s. A big smile dimpled her cheeks as she got ready to yell. Harry knowed we was excited, so he dragged it out.

"Are you ready for you $500 number?"

"Come on, Harry!" said Thelma. "Call my number."

Marie didn't pay no mind to Thelma. She was too busy inching down to the edge of her chair. I reached out and touched her arm, but she didn't even notice. Marie's eyes was glued to that red ball in Harry's hand.

"You old sorry sap-sucker, call my 0!"

Harry turned the ball toward Marie and announced, "The $500 number is 0 . . . 7 . . 4."

Thelma and Marie yelled, "Bingo!"

I grabbed Marie's arm and shook my head, "No." Marge jogged over to Thelma's table. Lucy switched over to our table, snatched Marie's card and called out, "Mistake! 0/75 wasn't called."

Lucy laughed, threw Marie's card back on the table and strutted back to the waitress station. Marge started calling back Thelma's numbers. And then Marie stood up. Her purse fell, opened. I could see the gun. I tried to pull her back into her seat but she wouldn't budge.

The gun jumped into Marie's hand. Her first shot blasted the food counter; Lucy ducked under the table, knocking donuts ever which way. The next bullet nicked Thelma's ear and she just silently slid outta her chair and passed out. I sat there watching the whole thing, too scared to move. I wet my pants.

Peoples was running like bats outta hell, screaming to wake the dead. Mattic Sampson was sitting closest to the exit door: she grabbed her coat and hit it. Mrs. Walker was sitting cross from me: she threw up Maalox. But didn't nobody try to stop Marie. Not even me.

And then Harry, he lost it, too. He was a pinball machine gone tilt, yelling into the mike, "Mistake! Please hold your cards. It's . . . it's a mistake!"

Marie shot at the numbers board. The lights behind numbers B/1 through O/74 burned out, but for some one-in-a-million reason, O/75 stayed lit. Marie shot again. Balls rolled across the floor, cracking as peoples knocked into each other, getting the hell outta Dodge. Harry kept yelling:

"Mistake. It's a mistake. Please hold your cards."

Bad a thought as it was, part of my brain said, "Don't forget to get Harry." But Marie messed up. She put the gun to her own head. I thought to myself, "Wait a minute, that ain't right." And then I grabbed out at her. I said, "Marie, Marie! I'll give you the money for your NSP bill. It ain't worth all this. Marie — "

I heard a blat. I couldn't move. I just couldn't. I was wet. Wet pee down my leg. Wet blood on my arm. Marie was red. No, her favorite color was red. Red clothes. Red shoes. Red blouse. Red trimmed cards. Red blood. Blood red running down her face.

Harry turned beet-red and screamed, "Mistake!" one more time before he flopped off his stool and fainted dead away. Weren't a mark on him. I swear I saw a red ball — an O — roll outta his sleeve as his head hit the floor. And then I yelled, "Aw, Lawd, Sweet Jesus, don't hold her to this. It's all a mistake." And it was. Cause Marie forgot to shoot Harry.

The Day We Discovered We Were Black

IT WASN'T REALLY Jo-Jo's fault. Honest it wasn't; if I'm lying, I'm flying. That Francis Scott Key man started the whole thing.

We got gypped in fourth grade, on the very first day of school. Mrs. Loving was sus-sposed to be our teacher and we'd been waiting for years to be in her class because she was the prettiest and nicest teacher in the whole school. Everybody knows when you're pretty you just have to be nice, so you know what ugly means. All the boys wanted to marry Mrs. Loving and all us girls wanted to look just like her, but by 8:05 that Monday morning, we learned that she had gone and spoiled everything by using up our summer having an old-bald-headed baby.

Our principal Mrs. Strickland, who we already didn't like in the first place, waddled into our classroom with this . . . this woman and announced that she was going to be our new teacher. Mrs. Strickland could have warned us in advance, mailed one of those yellow school bulletins she was so good at making up and safety-pinning to our coats at 3:30 so we wouldn't lose them on our way home from school. At least then we would've had the chance to change schools or something. We would've come back by fifth grade, honestly.

But we got sicked; what did I tell you about ugly? Those two women stood in Mrs. Loving's place behind the teacher's desk at the front of the room, the American flag hanging down almost to the tops of their heads, and they frowned at us because we were rolling our eyes at them.

We hadn't learned to be prejudiced or anything like that yet. Shoot, the closest some of us had ever come in touching range of living, breathing white people was the sales clerks downtown and they didn't count because we didn't know them personally. It wasn't that this Miss Fleischhacker was white and had a funny name that didn't sound like nothing we'd ever heard before. And shoot, it wasn't that she dressed so tacky, wearing all those old long dresses and shoes that curled up at the toes like a troll's or something's. It was just that she wasn't Mrs. Loving and we really, truly believed that Mrs. Strickland had done this to us on purpose because she hadn't ever liked our class. Well . . . sometimes we didn't mind our Ps and Qs, but even we didn't deserve this. So after Mrs. Strickland warned us to behave ourselves, and have a good year, she left us alone with this new teacher. Uumph, good year my foot.

We all had to stand up, one at a time, and tell her our names. We wouldn't've had to do that if Mrs. Loving had been our teacher, she knew who we were. And you could tell this teacher had been hipped to some of us – me and Jo-Jo and a couple of other kids, I won't say their names – by the way she looked at us when we said who we were, like she was taking Polaroids of us in her mind. I didn't like the way she looked at me when I stood up, put my hands on my hips and said, "My name is Denise Robinson."

This roll-call stuff took forever because she kept looking at us all cross-eyed, repeating our names after we told her who we were like she had a bad remembery or something. We couldn't forget her name. She wrote it on the blackboard in big chalky-white letters like we were blind or something, "My name is M I S S   F L E I S C H - H A C K E R," and told us about 50 zillion times how to pronounce it. I kept thinking to myself it was a shame for a kid to get hooked with a name like that, and boy was I glad I hadn't had anything like that happen to me.

The boys didn't want to marry her, and we girls surely didn't want to look like her:

M I S S   F L E I S C H H A C K E R had yellowed hair, and

yellowed teeth . . . with halitosis; her eyes were watery blue and she had a long pointy nose her glasses used for a sliding board; she didn't have no shape at all, just a bean pole. And after what she did to Jo-Jo we wondered how long we'd be in jail if we killed her. Here's 'zactly what happened – not on the first day of school, this was later in the year – and then you tell me who was wrong.

Our school has this thing called Morning Exercises. When the bell screeches at 8:00 a.m., the twenty of us slide out of our seats, place our right hands over our hearts, say the Pledge of Allegiance and then sing *The Star-Spangled Banner*. And we're usually good little poll-parrots, too, chirping the words in unison – that means all together. Everything kids do in school is in unison: singing, saying multiplication tables, not liking substitute teachers, getting in trouble, everything. And that morning we decided, in unison, to have some fun with old M I S S F L E I S C H H A C K E R.

So when the bell rang and she told us to take our places, we saluted the flag and chanted: "I pledge allegiance, to the flag, of the United States of America. And to the Republic, for which it stands. One nation, under God, invisible . . . "

"Stop!" said M I S S F L E I S C H H A C K E R, ratta-tat-ting on Mrs. Loving's desk with the yardstick. "The correct word is indivisible."

Shoot we knew that, even though we weren't real sure of what indivisible meant. We were just having a little bit of fun. The fifth grade kids told us they'd always had fun with Mrs. Loving last year, but old lady Fleischhacker wouldn't know fun if it was standing up on tip-toe right in front of her face.

"You will now start at the beginning, and recite the pledge properly this time or you will keep reciting it until you do say it correctly."

So we did it differently this time: "I pledge allegiance, to the flag, of the United States of America. And to the Republic, for which it stands, one nation, under God, IN-DI-VIS-A-BLE, with liberty and justice for all."

M I S S F L E I S C H H A C K E R didn't like it any better that way and since being a teacher means she could do whatever she wanted to do to us from 8:00 till 3:30, we backed down the third time around and said it the way she wanted us to. Not because we were ascared of her or anything like that; you may not like teachers, but you weren't ascared of them, even if your school did allow Corporal Punishment. We just said it the right way the third time because we figured if we didn't, this crazy old woman was just dumb enough to keep us standing up and pledging allegiance all day long. Some adults are like that you know, they'll hurt themselves just to get back at you.

As soon as we got through with liberty and justice for all, we made those cleaning-out-your-throat noises so we could launch into *The Star-Spangled Banner*. Oops, hold it, I forgot to tell you something. There were always two kids in charge of Morning Exercises: one kid held the flag and the other one directed the singing. The director had to give us our key, set the pitch if you wanta get technical about it. I don't know who that Francis Scott Key was thinking about when he wrote our national anthem, but he sure wasn't thinking about us.

I don't think old Francis was thinking about too many people at all because if you don't start singing that song in a low enough key, by the time you reach the "Rockets' red glare," you're into some notes it would take Grace Bumbry to reach. I know because she gave a concert at our school last year and I didn't know anybody could sing that high and still stay on key.

We didn't have any problems singing *Lift Every Voice and Sing*. Mr. James Weldon Johnson musta meant for anybody to sing his song, even little kids, because his notes were low enough so you could reach down in your guts and pull that song up through your throat and out your mouth like it was made for you. Wasn't no notes you could grab hold of. But I guess Francis Scott Key didn't want just anybody singing his song because he dangled his notes so high that little kids, and some adults, too, couldn't get a hold on them.

Anyway, up until fourth grade, whoever directed had always had enough sense to start us out on a real low note so we weren't squealing too bad by the time the rockets took off. But dumb old M I S S F L E I S C H H A C K E R, who was really pretty young to be honest about it, I guess – she just had some old ways about her – had the director use a pitch-pipe and we didn't know how to blow it too well. And that's what happened that day.

We started out too high and our voices cracked as we "Proudly held." We didn't have nowhere left to go when the rockets took off. It was really funny, you should've been there. Some kids kept trying to sing, some of us played charades with the words — Mrs. Loving's kids always played charades on Friday afternoons — but Jo-Jo started laughing. Real loud! At least he was being honest about it and not trying to fake the words. But fourth grade teachers like MISS FLEISCHHACKER don't want honesty, they just want you to sing when they tell you to. And Jo-Jo was cracking up.

Jo-Jo has one of those silly laughs, like a spastic pig snorting. And it was contagious, too, just like a sneeze or a yawn. We started giggling in unison. MISS FLEISCHHACKER ratta-tatted on Mrs. Loving's desk again which meant we were supposed to shut up. And normally we do. But that morning, Jo-Jo just wouldn't let us stop. I laughed so hard I caught the hiccups and thought to myself, "Shoot, the most she can make us do is re-sing it like she made us re-say the pledge." So I kept laughing and hiccuping. We all kept laughing and MISS FLEISCHHACKER kept beating on the desk.

She kept on beating on the desk, harder and harder, and I really looked at her for a change. I usually spent most of my time doing my work, trying to ignore her. But when her face started changing colors, I stopped hiccupping right in the middle of a hic. Something was cracking her friendly-teacher's-mask into little tiny pieces, and whatever it was, MISS FLEISCHHACKER aimed it directly at Jo-Jo.

I got ascared then, just a little bit though because the most she could do was smack Jo-Jo on his open palm five times with the yardstick and he was used to getting corporally punished. But all of a sudden the classroom was loud with quietness; everybody else had stopped laughing and looked ascared, too. All nineteen of us just stood there and watched MISS FLEISCHHACKER and Jo-Jo.

Poor old Jo-Jo has one of those laughs that just has to die out on its own, so I'm not real sure if he ever saw her coming. But we did and somebody tugged at his sleeve, trying to get him to shut up. He still couldn't stop laughing. Jo-Jo snorted and honked right up untill MISS FLEISCHHACKER slapped him across the face and called him a nigger.

I rubbed my cheek, that's how much I knew it hurt Jo-Jo. MISS FLEISCHHACKER walked back to Mrs. Loving's desk and said, "You will now start from the beginning and show respect for our national anthem. Ready . . . begin."

It was just pitiful. Some kids started crying; some kids tried to sing. But Jo-Jo called her the "b" word! I know that was wrong but we'd eavesdropped in on the big kids one day and bitch rhymed with witch and titty rhymed with kitty and a cherry didn't always go on top of a chocolate sundae, except we couldn't figure that one out until Jo-Jo snuck a Playboy to school one day — and I'm still not sure I get it. We knew Jo-Jo had called her something bad but she had no business slapping him like that and calling him that word our parents said you never call anybody, even if you're just playing.

I didn't understand what was going on. We'd always laughed whenever we missed that note and all we ever had to do before this woman came to our school was re-sing it, starting in a lower key. So she didn't have to slap his face like that — the Corporal Punishment Rulebook didn't say you could. I couldn't wait to get home and tell my parents all about it. And just when I thought everything was all over, M I S S F L E I S C H H A C K E R walked back to Jo-Jo's desk and back-handed him for calling her something I bet you anything she was being.

Some kids fell into their chairs. Some of us kept standing up and stared at her, crying. A few kids found somebody's pitch and started singing. Netta, the girl who had been holding the flag, ran outta the classroom, tripped down to the principal's office and sent the assistant principal, Mrs. Warden, running down the hallway to see what was happening. Netta was too petrified-stiff to come back so she laid down on a cot in the office until her mother could take off work and pick her up.

Mrs. Warden took M I S S F L E I S C H H A C K E R by the arm and pulled her into the hallway. Didn't nobody say a word except Jo-Jo. He wasn't crying or anything, just standing there with two rocket-red-glaring cheeks and saying the "B" word, over and over and over.

And that's when we divided the world up into black people and white people. All of our teachers had been black until fourth grade, and whenever they'd corporally punished us we knew we were being paddled for our own good. They'd always said it hurt them more than it hurt us — I wondered about that sometimes when I was waiting for my hand to stop stinging. They told us we were good kids who sometimes did bad things, but that they loved us. And they never called us names, even if Netta was a cry-baby and you-know-who was a rubber-butt.

But M I S S   F L E I S C H H A C K E R was white, and she had called Jo-Jo a nigger and slapped him in the face, twice, just because she was mad at him for laughing about something funny. He wasn't laughing at her or anything she had said or done. Jo-Jo had laughed because we sounded silly trying to sing a song I don't think old Francis Scott Key meant for us to sing in the first place or he would have put the notes closer for us to reach. Jo-Jo had laughed during a Morning Exercise full of big words we didn't understand, like indivisible.

But we understood pain and embarrassment and scarediness. And after our new-new fourth grade teacher explained why we had Morning Exercises and what the Pledge of Allegiance really meant, we finally understood that indivisible was like singing in unison. So we decided, indivisibly, not to be too happy or laugh at anything for the rest of the year, even though M I S S   F L E I S C H - H A C K E R never came back.

We had long talks with our parents. We talked to the school psycho-logicalist. And we still wondered what people like M I S S   F L E I S C H H A C K E R would do, and could do to us, if we ever did something they really didn't like.

Unpaid Debts

DON'T EVER BORROW anything from her in your life. Ever. I don't care how broke you are. Not that borrowing is a habit of mine, but she collects debts with a passion. I've known her for about twenty years now, so I'm speaking from experience. We're not really friends, more like associates if you understand the difference. She doesn't have any friends, but she owns quite a few associates.

Let me try and explain. Tina, Lisa, Pam, and I were partying at the Elks, looking good, feeling good, having a good time. Not a great time, just a dateless kind of Saturday night time. I was dancing with a man whose line wasn't too full of it – at least he didn't call me "Hey, momma," or "Hey, sister," or Hey any other member of his extended family. After he sweated and stomped on my toes, through an extended version of Kool and the Gang, he escorted me back to the table because it was on his way to the bar.

I knew I wouldn't have to see him again until 1:00 a.m. when he would ask me if I needed a ride home. Unfortunately I've become all too familiar with that line: it has a tendency to tuck dateless Saturday nights into bed. Pam had ordered drinks while I was on the floor with Mr. We-Can-Throw-Down-Baby, and I laughed along with them about my latest conquest, sipping Pepsi like it was a rum-and-coke. But as I was saying, we were having a good enough time. Good enough until we heard a loud, mannish voice yell, "Paula! Hey, girlfriend, whatcha doing here?"

Pam looked disgusted and, being careful to keep her voice down, said, "We're doing the same thing we do every Saturday night, sitting here drinking Pepsis and waiting for rides home. What the hell does she think we're doing?"

Tina said, "Do we have to run into her everywhere we go?" while Lisa decided it was a good time to freshen her make-up and escaped to the ladies' room.

Mu'Lee, the woman I'm telling you about, was bulldozing her way toward our table, yelling, "Hey, so-and-so," at people trying to pretend they didn't hear her. She invited herself to join us, sprawled gap-legged into Lisa's chair, glared at me and announced to everyone within earshot, "Paula, didn't I let you borrow that dress TWO YEARS AGO!"

Now let's get this straight. In the first place she didn't let me borrow that dress, she had given it to me. Mu'Lee knew she couldn't fit it when she bought it. And in the second place, the only reason she bought it was she knew I wanted it. Never mind the fact that she was wearing my used-to-be favorite necklace, surrendered after three days of, "Girlfriend, you know you oughta gimme that thing. You still owe me for those greens I bought you at the Farmer's Market last week."

I could have reminded her that she helped me eat those greens when she came over to dinner last Sunday, but why waste my breath. The greens had nothing to do with anything. The important thing at that moment was Mu'Lee wanted everyone to know she had given me the dress. I was used to her pulling this number by now, so I just sat there consoling myself with the thought that the Elks closed in an hour.

Muzetta Lee Cotton is something else. I've always called her Mu'Lee for short, at her request, and I don't suppose I have to tell you what other people call her, behind her back of course. She was born in some little town down South that either she never named or I simply don't remember. All I seem to recall is her mentioning her six brothers and four sisters, or is it the other way around— whatever, I know she comes from a big family.

Mu'Lee could be an attractive woman if she'd pay more attention to her appearance but she doesn't even try. I've tried talking her into getting a perm but she still styles her hair in that same short afro she was wearing the day we met. Mu'Lee has healthy dark brown skin, with glimmering red undertones, and could really enhance her looks if she would simply apply a little make-up: a dab of foundation, a little concealer here and there, and just a hint of blush and eyeshadow wouldn't hurt either. I've told her girdles are a lot more comfortable now that the staves have been removed: even Playtex uses lycra and spandex these days. If Mu'lee spent just a little more time worrying about her appearance, and less time worrying about people owing her, she would have the friends she claims she wants.

I've told her, "You can't buy friends, even on your income." And Mu'Lee does make good money. Good enough to keep the bookkeeping department from deducting the three dollar a month service charge from her savings account for falling below a minimum monthly balance. Her checks don't bounce and she has more plastic than Tupperware. If she's ever heard of generics, you'd never guess it; her whole house is a brand name: Singer, Hoover, Curtis Mathis, Whirlpool – you name it, she has it. Need any missing ingredient for dinner tonight? She has it. Mu'Lee has enough Green Giant, Campbells and Del Monte in storage to last a year.

"Sure, girlfriend, come on over and get it. I keeps that stuff on the shelf. Never know when somebody may need something.

"After all, girlfriend," – I wish she'd stop calling me that, it doesn't sound proper coming from another woman – " if you don't have nothing other folks want, then you ain't got nothing to let them borrow. And if they don't borrow nothing, then they can't owe you nothing and you can't get nothing outta them."

The interest on her generosity isn't any more than an embarrassment or two. She'll talk about whatever she loaned you long after you've repaid her, making sure to buy sixty-nine cent a can Hunts, rather than three-for-a-dollar Monarch. Sometimes I feel like no matter what I do, I'll always owe her, I'll owe her for the rest of my life.

I suppose some people would say I sound snotty, selfish. I don't worry about that, Mu'Lee has said the same thing from time to time. And I suppose the same people would say that if I dislike Mu'Lee so much, why don't I just stop associating with her. Well, did you ever hear me say I disliked her? I just don't like some of the things she does. But to understand why I can't just stop seeing her altogether, you'll have to know how we met.

I was seventeen, sitting on a bench waiting for the bus, when this woman flounced up and plopped down right next to me.

"Girl . . ." — she started out calling me girl, the girlfriend didn't come until later — "I know the bus is late, but crying ain't gonna get it here no sooner. What's the matter with you, girl?"

I could tell she was older, but I thought she had a nerve calling me "girl." And when you're seventeen years old, crying at the bus stop, trying to build up the courage to run away from home, the last thing you need is someone asking you, "What's the matter?" You can't tell a complete stranger your period is three weeks late and you're too scared to go to the doctor. So I scooted over to the edge of the bench and tried to ignore her.

She didn't get the hint and slid next to me saying, "Girl, whatever it is, it can't be all that bad."

Tears make fools of themselves when someone pats you lightly on the shoulder. Before I could stop myself I blurted out, "No period . . . scared to see doc . . . can't tell Mom . . . don't want . . . baby."

"Okay, girl, calm down. Let's see what we can do 'bout this. There's a park over yonder. You ain't in no shape to take no bus nowhere."

We went to the park as the bus drove by.

"That's better. Here, blow your nose. Okay now?"

"A little," I said. "Thanks. I'm sorry. I mean . . . I —"

"I know. My name's Muzetta, Muzetta Lee Cotton. But all my friends call me Mu'Lee. What's your name?"

"Paula. Paula Harris."

"Well, hi there, Paula. Let's see what we can figger out to do."

"Thanks, but I'm all right now. I'd better be going." I tried to walk away from her.

"I can see yo' momma told you don't never talk to no strangers, girl, but talking's ain't what got you in trouble, is it?" Mu'Lee laughed.

It wasn't a ha-ha-ha-you're-in-trouble laugh. It was more of a I'd-cry-too-if-it-would-help-but-it-won't-so-calm-down laugh. I realized that a couple of days later, but at that moment all I wanted was to get away from this Muzetta Lee Cotton, who knew more about me than my parents did.

"Really, I'm okay now. I might not even be pregnant – I'm just late. So . . . so I'll just wait and see. I better go now. Nice meeting you. Bye."

Mu'Lee grabbed my arm and pulled herself off the grass as she asked me, "You ever been late before?"

"No!" I said, thinking to myself, why doesn't she leave me alone?

"Tell you what. Since you scared to go to the doctor, go home and take a birth control pill and some castor oil. If you pregnant, it'll slide on out. You got some birth control pills at home?"

I wanted to scream, "If I had some birth control pills, I wouldn't maybe be pregnant, would I?" What I said was, "Where in the world did you hear something silly like that?"

"Look, girl, down where I come from, we didn't go to no doctors, couldn't afford to. Miss Lonnie knew how to take care of us, 'cluding what's wrong with you. I got six brothers and four sisters and ain't none of us ever had anything Miss Lonnie couldn't fix.

"You standing there looking at me all funny but, girl, I know. I'm just trying to help you out. Now go on home, take you a pill and a big tablespoon of castor oil and everything'll be fine."

I wanted to hit her. Run, scream, anything but listen to this nonsense. "I don't have any damn pills!" I said.

"That's okay," Mu'Lee said as she pulled a pink vinyl case out of her purse. "Take one of mine."

I told her, "It's dangerous to take someone else's medicine."

"It's dangerous having a baby, too. Look, girl, here's my number. You ain't gotta call me, you ain't gotta see me no more. Nobody even gotta know we talked about this. But if you wanna call me later on, I'll be up. Call me."

I went home and took a birth control pill and a big tablespoon of castor oil. My period started the next morning. A week later, although I have absolutely no idea why, I called Mu'Lee.

"I was just calling to thank you."

"Girl, I told you it would work," she said.

"I don't know if it worked or not, but my period started."

Mu'Lee said, "It worked!"

I didn't want to argue about it and was beginning to feel sorry I'd ever called her. But since I was trying to be polite I said, "If there's ever anything I can do for you –"

Mu'Lee pounced on my words. "Oh, girl, don't worry about it. You owe me one."

I didn't realize that I'd owe her one for the rest of my life.

That fall, Pam, Lisa, Tina, and I began attending college. We were going to become famous: Pam was majoring in dramatic arts, Lisa in music, Tina in Pre-Law Males 101 and I, in studio arts. While I was studying to become a success, Mu'Lee made money.

I'd go visit her on the weekends, sometimes taking my friends along with. Mu'Lee never minded, she enjoyed our company. We'd give parties at her house and one night as we were decorating her basement, I asked why she never invited her friends over. "I know we're a few years younger, but we're pretty mature for our ages."

All she ever said was, "I see my friends all week at work, girl. Don't need them around on the weekends, too. It's fun having y'all around, keeping me company, having some girl talk."

She fed us her homemade peach cobbler, and floated us small loans from time to time, which we repaid out of our allowances. We told her all about our lives. She never seemed to want to talk about hers, so we didn't ask.

Sometimes Mu'Lee and I would meet at Field's for lunch and afterwards I'd try on dresses I knew I couldn't afford.

"Mu'Lee, just feel this. Don't you just love the feel of silk against your skin? It's so sexy!"

She would sigh and say, "Girl, I can't wear nothing like this to work."

"You don't wear something like this to work, silly. It's for special occasions, like last minute dinner invitations."

"I don't get no last minute dinner invitations, don't you know? But it do look good on you. Why don't you get it?"

"I have to buy some oil paints when we leave here, remember? I don't need that dress, anyway . . . not really. It's as much fun trying clothes on as buying them. Anything else you want to look at, I'm running kind of late?"

"No, girl. I'll drive you back to school. C'mon."

Two weeks later I had a one-woman exhibit at the University Gallery. I asked Mu'Lee if she wanted to attend but she just looked at me the way she does when I tell her she can invite her friends to our parties at her house.

"No, girl, I don't go to things like that. Whatcha gonna wear?"

I thought about it a minute and said, "I don't know yet. I'll probably grab something out of the closet. Are you sure you wouldn't like to go?"

Ignoring the question, Mu'Lee tole me to follow her into the spare bedroom. "Girl, I thought 'bout what you said 'bout them last minute dinner invitations, so I went back to Field's and bought this thing. Got it home and the damn thing don't fit."

She opened the closet door and pulled out the silk dress I had tried on. "Mu'Lee," I said, "how many times do I have to tell you to try on dresses before you buy them? Now you'll have to take it back to the store and either exchange it for a bigger size or get a refund."

"Girl, I don't have time to keep running downtown, trying stuff on and taking it back. Here, you wanna wear it tonight?"

I tried to explain it to her. "You can't take the dress back after you've worn it."

"Tell you what, girl. You go ahead and wear it to your thing at the university. No big deal, you'll owe me one."

Mu'Lee smiled as she draped the dress across my arm. The exhibit was a success and I received quite a few compliments on my dress. The night was so exciting, I didn't think about Mu'Lee much. I supposed she did whatever she does when I'm not around.

Two years later my parents were killed in a car accident. Mu'Lee saw to all the funeral arrangements and I moved in with her until I married Roger. She cooked for me, washed and ironed my clothes, and this was when she switched from calling me "girl" to "girlfriend." I loved the attention and she loved my company. My friends came over to visit, often; hers didn't. Mu'Lee always made everyone feel right at home – even Roger. And even though I could tell she didn't like him very much, she loaned him money sometimes. My debts were beginning to pile up.

I married Roger when I was twenty-five years old, six months after we met. Pam's husband, Bill, had introduced us at their wedding and we seemed to hit it off right away. My artwork wasn't selling and I was beginning to think about other career options even though Mu'Lee kept saying I was giving up too soon, that you never fail unless you stop trying. That was all well and good for her to say, she had a good job and money in the bank.

"But, girlfriend, I'm working at the job I want. I'm good at what I do and you're supposed to make money when you work hard. But you want things to fall it in yo' lap, like you think somebody owes you something, and life just ain't that way. Marrying Roger ain't gonna change that. You sure you know what you getting yo'self into?"

"Of course I know what I'm getting into. I love Roger and he loves me."

"Something 'bout him I don't trust. He's a friend of Pam's Bill, ain't he?"

I think Pam and Bill must have owed her some money because there was a hardness in her voice whenever she mentioned them.

I tried to laugh it off by saying, "You're acting jealous, Mu'Lee. You don't have to worry, you're not losing me. I'll still come over to Sunday dinner. And it's not really Roger, is it? I can't think of one man I've ever dated that you liked."

"That's 'cause you keep dating them same kinda no good men."

That did it. I'd had enough of her judgmental attitude. So I said, "I'm going to marry Roger whether you like it or not."

"It's your bed . . ."

"And I can't wait to sleep in it!"

After all our arguing, Mu'Lee helped organize my wedding. I didn't ask her to be one of my attendants because she didn't like Pam and Bill anymore, and since they were going to be our matron of honor and best man, well . . . you can understand, can't you? Mu'Lee didn't care; she bought herself a lilac mother-of-the-bride dress, escorted herself down the aisle to the front pew and cried through the service.

Not long after my wedding Mu'Lee started her buying sprees. Roger and I went to her house for Sunday dinners and he noticed it before I did. Roger never missed anything.

"Hey, Paula," he asked, "why the hell does that old mule—"

"Her name is Mu'Lee—"

"Right . . . Mu'Lee. Why the hell does she keep buying stuff she never uses? Did you see that stereo equipment? All those records and you know she never plays them."

"It's her money. She can spend it any way she wants."

"Yeah. People who don't know what to do with it always have money."

I thought to myself, "If this isn't a case of the pot talking about the kettle. If you'd stop spending our money as fast as I make it—"

"—We could use a stereo like that. Why don't you ask her for it. She'll give you anything and you know it."

"I can't ask her for her stereo. Borrowing money in an emergency is one thing – we always pay her back and we wouldn't have to do that if you'd stay away from the track – "

"Shut up," he yelled. "You like spending money as well as I do. And don't think I don't know your girlfriend" – he could make that word sound so nasty – "slips you money on the side. Look, tell her we'll buy it from her. It'll be cheaper than buying it new. Do it for me, Paula."

Roger pulled me against him and without going into it here, let's just say we got the stereo. And the microwave, and the VCR, and more money. I became as sick of Roger's wanting as I was of Mu'Lee's giving. Sick of us owing her; sick of feeling I would always owe her something. Feeling the same way I felt the day we met on that bus stop. I wanted to escape from her as much as I wanted to leave Roger. And he felt the same way. After withdrawing everything from our joint bank account, he left me. At least I didn't owe him anything anymore.

When I told Mu'Lee that Roger and I were divorcing, I expected a little bit of sympathy. What Mu'Lee said was, "Girlfriend, that's not surprising. Men always leave you in a mess."

My throat began to itch. "What's that supposed to mean?"

"You know good and damn well what that means. We met 'cause a man left you in a mess, remember?"

There had always been an unspoken agreement between us to never mention that incident. All that happened years ago and I never did believe in that birth control and castor oil concoction, anyway.

I said, "I don't want to talk about that."

"I know you don't. There's lots of things you don't wanna talk 'bout, ain't there? You only wanna talk to me when you wanna talk, don't you?"

I yelled back at her, "What's that supposed to mean?"

"It means, girlfriend, from the day I met you, I tried to be yo' friend. I let you and yo' high-society friends come around here and have yo' parties. I let y'all borrow money – "

"We paid you back!"

"Some things you can't never pay back. I didn't need no money, I needed you to be my friend."

Mu'Lee looked as angry as I felt.

"I was your friend," I said. "You act like I was the only friend you ever had."

35

"Did you ever see me with any other friends?"

"I don't work with you, do I? What about all your friends at work?"

"Girlfriend, you may have went to college but you ain't nothing but an educated fool. Did you ever see me with any friends from work?"

I didn't want to hear any more of this, didn't want to know what it implied. I should have just left it alone, but I didn't. I said, "Well, whose fault is that?"

Mu'Lee glared at me. I could feel hatred radiating from her body; her face convulsed. She said, "Bitch! You owed it to me to be my friend. Didn't they learn you anything at that fancy school of yo's besides how to paint pictures? You and Roger used me, and that damn Pam and her Bill and all the others, too. You all used me."

I exploded. "You're the one ignorant enough to let people use you. Roger used everybody but I never used you. I always paid you back. And whatever Pam and Bill and anyone else did to you, I don't know anything about that — "

"You didn't want to know — "

"Shut up! If anybody used you, it's your own damn fault. You can't buy friends."

"I bought you!"

I hated her then. "Well, I'm not your friend now, and I won't ever be again. You don't own me."

I turned my back on her as she said, "You can leave here if you want to. Go 'head, get the hell out. But you'll be back. You'll need me long before I'll ever . . . ever need you. You'll always owe me."

Mu'Lee was right. We needed each other, and that need has done some ugly things to who we are. We inched back together, making up rules for our relationship as we went along. She gave and I accepted; I repaid and she gave more. Before our fight, the transactions remained private. But now she took great pleasure from publicly announcing, "Didn't I give you that dress, TWO YEARS AGO?"

"Don't you still owe me THREE DOLLARS from last week?"

"You still wearing that hat I gave you? I'm surprised the feather still looks THAT GOOD."

I put up with it. I'm not a famous artist. I'm not anything but a divorced nine-to-fiver just like Pam and Lisa and Tina. Mu'Lee and

I still have dinner together on Sundays. Last week we ate fried chicken and greens and cornbread that she bought and I cooked.

Dinner will be at my apartment next Sunday. Then we'll go downtown and see a movie. I owe her an outing since she took me to a concert I wanted to attend last month — Mu'Lee could afford the tickets. And then the week after that, she'll do something else for me and I'll return the favor. And things will go on and on like that until the day I die. But even then Mu'Lee will stand over my grave and tell me I can't leave her: because I owe her one.

Three Alarm Fire

I ONLY DID IT cause I thought it would make mommy happy for once. Then maybe she'd quit picking on people all the time. Always screaming at my daddy about we don't have no money, so she can't buy no new clothes from the real store with the pretend ladies in the window. I like shopping at the G OD ILL, even if it do look like an old snaggletooth tiger cause some of the letters are missing.

Nice people know little bitty five-year-old girls like me need dresses and shoes and toys. So when their little girls get too big, nice people take their stuff to the G OD ILL so daddies can borrow them and bring them home to me. Daddy says we have to take the clothes back when I get too big so the next little girl can have something new to wear. Daddy is nice people, too.

Mommy wants real-store bought clothes. And a shiny car like Uncle Billy's, with a top that folds down like a 'cordian so she can let her hair loose and everybody can see it blowing in the breeze. I know mommy likes people to see her with her hair down, 'cepting I not posed to tell.

Know how I know?

Cause when my daddy goes to work Uncle Billy comes over, pulls the bobby pins outta mommy's hair and it falls over her shoulders like Rapunzel's. Then her and Uncle Billy go into my daddy's bedroom and lock the door so they can watch T.V. I guess Uncle Billy don't hear too good so mommy turns the sound up really really loud.

Mommy's always talking about leaving me and daddy. One time after I finished saying my, "Now I lay me down to sleeps," I saw a star-light, star-bright and wished I may, wished I might, that mommy would disappear that night. But I quit doing that after what happened the next day.

Mommy woke up screaming at people. She yelled the divorce word at my daddy, and then slammed the door when she left. I thought my wish was coming true cause I knew that word meant she wasn't coming home no more. That was okey-dokey, I was used to taking care of me, myself. And I could take care of my daddy, too. But when I climbed up in his lap and told him so, my daddy hugged me real, real, real tight and started crying.

I didn't know daddies cried. I know they "Ha-ha-haed" when they read their little girls Dr. Seuss; they jumped off the couch yelling, "Back . . . back . . . back . . . HOMERUN!" when the baby bears hit the ball outta the park; they wrinkled their faces and said, "Not in front of the baby," when mommy started yelling if I was in the room with them. Sometimes, but not too many sometimeses, they made funny noises at night when they were in the bedroom with mommy and I woke up cause they were knocking on the bedroom wall, but when I went to see what they wanted, they wouldn't let me in so I sat down by the door and listened.

And they always told their little girls they loved them when they tucked them into bed at night. But I never knew daddies cried. And I never wished mommy would disappear, again. At least not to the star-light, star-bright, even though he was the only one who listened to me. I just hoped daddy wasn't crying cause he thought I couldn't take care of him. I could.

Know how I knew I could?

One time I told my mommy I was hungry and she told me to go fix me something to eat. I was going to fix me a hot dog, but the fire wouldn't come on when I turned the knob on the stove marked "F." I said, "Mommy, the fire blew itself out."

"Then make yourself a sandwich and leave me alone, Cissy. Can't you see I'm trying to sleep?"

Mommy was always tired when Uncle Billy left our house. Said she needed her beauty sleep. It worked, too, cause my mommy is pretty. She has long ruby-red hair, just like me. And green eyes, just like me. One time I heard Uncle Billy joking with mommy, saying, "Momma's baby, poppa's maybe." I didn't like him too much after that cause I was my daddy's baby. So I asked my granny — who's got red hair and green eyes, too — about it. Granny looked like she didn't like Uncle Billy too much either when she told me, "Of course he's your daddy, Cissy. Don't pay no attention to people who can't find nothing better to do than meddle in other people's business."

I always felt better after I talked to granny, but she didn't visit us too much. I didn't have nobody to talk to but star-light, star-bright, even though mommy was home all day. Mommy didn't like to talk to me.

Mommy's short, but she's taller than me. She liked it when people said, "Caroline Fairchild, you look young enough to be Cissy's older sister rather than her mother." But she was my mommy, and mommies were 'posed to feed their little girls when they were hungry. I may look like her but I'm going to stay home all day and cook for my children when I grow up. I told her, again, "Mom . . . my. I don't want a jelly bread sammich. I want a hot dog."

"All right, dammit! I'm only going to show you how to do this one time, so you better pay attention. Get in here."

I followed her to the kitchen. She jerked a drawer open and pulled out the long box of matches. I backed up when she did that and said, "Mommy, Big Bird said that little kids not 'posed to play with matches."

"Then tell Big Bird to cook your hot dog. Look, Cissy, all you have to do is hold the box in this hand . . . here, hold it — Now hold the stick in your other hand . . . like this — Now drag the stick along the black side of the box — Harder, Cissy, harder."

The stick caught on fire after one, two, three strikes you're out and flashed so brightly, I dropped it on the floor. Mommy started screaming at me:

"What the hell are you trying to do, burn the damn house down?"

But then she got this funny look on her face and started laughing. Mommy looked 'specially pretty when she smiled. I wish she smiled all the time.

"On second thought, maybe that's not such a bad idea. Burn this rat-trap down to the ground — it's insured. That'd be one way of getting some money."

"If the house burned down we'd get some money, mommy?"

"Isn't that what I just said? I could buy my car and a new wardrobe and — "

Mommy started making up an out-loud grocery list of all the things she could buy for herself if our house burned down. She looked so happy, I decided to ask the star-light, star-bright about it.

"No use daydreaming about it. If it weren't for bad luck I'd have no luck at all. This lousy house will be standing long after I'm dead and gone. I'm so goddamn tired of being poor. I wish that just one time in my life I could have something I want. Just one time — "

I was used to mommy forgetting I was somewhere and talking to herself. I could have told her your dreams only come true if you dream them at night. But she never asked me. So I kept practicing lighting matches. Then she remembered I was in the kitchen with her.

"Will you stop doing that before you use up all the matches. After you get it lit, put it over the pilot — "

"The what?"

"The pi . . . this little hole right here, and watch. See the blue flame? Now you know the stove is working. Turn on the burner and see."

When I turned the knob marked "F" this time, blue fire came out each hole of the burner, one piece at a time the way flower petals open in the spring.

"All right, Cissy, put the hot dogs in the pan and let them boil until they start looking fat. Then turn them off, take the pan over to the sink, pour out the hot water, and use the long fork to pick them up with. You understand? And don't you dare tell your father I taught you how to light matches."

"I won't tell, mommy, promise."

And I didn't have my fingers crossed behind my back when I said it. I was so happy mommy and I had a secret, plus besides, now I knew how to cook. It was easy. Boiling just meant you let the water get good and mad and bubble itself like it does when you fart in the bath tub, only faster. Like when mommy says she's boiling mad if I wake her up or bother her when the soapy operas are on.

Plus besides that, there's another reason why I wouldn't tell daddy me and mommy's secret. Me and daddy had a secret, too, and I wouldn't tell her it cause I knew she would take it away from me. The secret is: I know all about fire.

Know how I know?

Cause sometimes, when mommy goes out at night, daddy and me follow her. Daddy says, "We just want to make sure nothing happens to mommy when she's out by herself, don't we, Cissy?"

I didn't really want nothing to happen to mommy, but I knew nothing would. Cause most of the time when we saw her, she was with Uncle Billy. So daddy didn't have nothing to worry about, Uncle Billy would take good care of her. I went with daddy cause of the other things.

When mommy wasn't in the car — our top didn't fold down but I liked it anyway — I got to ride up front with daddy, in mommy's seat. Daddy looked good in the dark insides of the car. He was darker than me and mommy and his skin shined when we drove under the street lamps that lit everything up when the sun went to bed at night. Daddy was so tall his head almost reached the top of the car when he sat down to drive. He had big arms and legs that twitched when he walked or carried me on his back. Twitched like his face did whenever we saw mommy with Uncle Billy. And daddy always smelled so good. I liked riding around with him at night.

After we made sure mommy was safe, daddy would take me to Dairy Queen and buy me a dip-cone, strawberry. And a lot of times we'd stop and watch fires on our way home. Seems like something was always on fire around our house. Daddy would park the car and carry me piggy-back to watch, ice cream sliding down my arm into his hair.

It was hot where the fire was. Daddy would be so hot he'd start sweating and I got hot being held in his arms. His heart would thumpity-thump real real real fast and mine almost kept up. It would be so hot it was hard to catch your breath cause even the air was hot. It was exciting watching the long red fire tongues licking up the buildings just like the way I licked up strawberry ice cream. The faster the fire licked, the faster I licked; the building melted right along with my cone. And daddy would hold me even tighter.

That was me and daddy's secret, even after one of his friends tried to take it away from us one night. We were watching a house burn down and a man walked up to daddy and said, "Julian, you oughta be ashamed of yourself – bringing a baby out to see something like this. What if worse comes to worse and people get hurt? You want your baby to see that?"

I told the man, "You leave my daddy alone."

Daddy said, "You take care of your family and I'll take care of mine. I wouldn't let anything in the world happen to my baby girl and you can take that to the bank."

The man looked at my daddy and said, "Look, I know what's going on with you, man – and I'm sorry. But dragging your child out at night just so you can follow her – "

"Chill out! Cissy and I just came out for a bit of fresh air and an ice cream. Right, baby girl?"

I said, "Uh-huh. But we made sure mommy was safe first, didn't we, daddy?"

Daddy didn't answer me. He just watched the man watching us. Looking at me, then looking at daddy. Then the man shook his head and said, "Julian, we've been buddies for a long time and I wouldn't tell you nothing wrong. But you've got to get some help for all three of you before something happens."

I'd never seen daddy really mad until he yelled, "Stay the hell out of my business," at the man. People were watching us more than they were watching the fire. I heard one lady say, "That poor little thing," and wondered how she knew we were poor.

Before the man walked away he patted me on my head and said, "Try and take care of yourself, honey." When I told him I always took care of myself he said he bet I did.

On the way home I asked daddy what worse came to worse meant.

"Don't let that man worry you, baby girl. He wasn't talking about us. All he meant was sometimes fires get out of control and people get hurt."

"But I thought the fireman climbed up the ladders and carried everybody out piggyback, like you do with me?"

"They do, if they get there in time – "

"Why wouldn't they get there in time?"

"Well, Cissy, nobody knows when there's going to be a fire. Most fires are accidents and the firemen can't come until someone sees the building burning and calls them."

"But what if the firemen knew there was going to be a fire."

"How could they know, baby girl?"

"I don't know." And I didn't cause I hadn't figgered that out yet. But I would. So I asked daddy something else.

"Do people get money when their houses burn up, daddy?"

"They do if they have insurance – "

"A lot of money? Enough to buy a new car and new clothes and make mom . . . people happy?"

"What did you say, Cissy? Make who happy? Why all the questions, baby?"

"Nothing, daddy. I just heard some of the people who were watching the fire with us talking and some of them said, 'Well, they'll get a new house now.' So I was just wondering – "

I could get like mommy sometimes: forget daddy was somewhere and start talking to myself. That's what I had been doing, talking to myself, cause I didn't hear nothing daddy said . . . not really. But I could feel lots of words moving around in my head, trying to find a place to hide. I'd get star-light, star-bright to find them.

And sure enough, next week star-light, star-bright told me what to do. I knew how to dial 911. It was easy cause the numbers on our phone lit up in the dark. I told my best friend that my real-store bought dolly, Sad-Eyes, never got to go anywhere and wanted to visit her dollies. So my friend took Sad-Eyes home with her. Now I was almost ready.

Mommy told me I had been a good girl all week cause I had let her get her beauty sleep without waking her up even once. But she wasn't as tired as she used to be since Uncle Billy had left town. I'd heard her tell one of her friends that she hadn't known daddy was that much of a man. I didn't understand mommy – didn't she know daddy was a man? But I didn't have time to think about it that much cause I had been busy practicing.

It was nice to hear her say, "You've been such a good girl, mommy's going to try and do something nice for you."

"I'm going to do something nice for you, too."

"Really, Cissy? What are you going to do for mommy?"

"I can't tell you cause it's a secret. But it will make you really really happy."

I loved her when she was smiling. Even daddy was smiling a lot more than he used to. I don't know why, but all three of us were happy at the same time and I was going to make sure things stayed that way. Cause all that was important was keeping mommy and daddy happy.

Star-light, star-bright said it was time. I knew they were asleep cause I listened through their bedroom door and didn't hear nothing but snoring noises. I tippy-toed downstairs to the kitchen and opened the drawer. Then I tippy-toed into the living room and put the phone on the end-table by the side of the couch.

I had practiced real good. The match lighted up the first time I dragged it across the black side of the box. But the couch wouldn't act right; it blew the fire out when I put the pillow over it. So I lit another match. The couch blew that one out, too. The next time, I laid the match on top of the pillow and that worked just fine.

It burned real real real slow at first. So I lit another match to help it out. Then another one, then another one. The last one helped out so much I had to get up off the couch. The fire was starting up. It wasn't as pretty as the fires daddy had taken me to yet, but it was still exciting. It was just that everything else was going wrong.

My eyes were stinging so much it was hard to see the numbers on the phone even though they were lighted up. Then the living room got real smoky and it was hard to see anything at all. I remembered the man on the T.V. said if a fire was chasing you to drop on your knees and crawl – so I did. I crawled away from the phone.

I don't remember too much after that cause I kept falling asleep and waking up. And dreaming. One time I dreamed daddy was holding me in his arms: we were hot, sweaty. Then I dreamed mommy was screaming at people. But she hadn't screamed at people since Uncle Billy left town, so that couldn't be right. The screaming stopped. It started again.

I woke up one more time before I went back to sleep. I had a feeling I was outside but it didn't seem so cold to me. Not cold enough for my mommy and daddy to throw the blankets over their heads.

Then I looked up and saw the star-light, star-bright winking at me, and I knew I would get my wish. I couldn't wait until we moved into our new house.

The Dietary Exploits of Bessie

(A Fable)

It says so on page 54: you burn up 7-8 calories per minute doing heavy duty exercises. If that's the case, the way Sweet Meat was bumping and grinding and getting on down with it, sweating over Bessie and her blue satin sheets like a chocolate brown M-and-M melting in your mouth not in your hand, he'd already evaporated 315 calories. That would just about make a dent in those Sloe Screws he consummated down at the Club. But Sweet Meat'd still need some hours to work off that rib-tib dinner and Bessie'd be damned if she was gonna be his trampoline much longer seeing as how he wasn't the one on a diet. She was. So she just lay there like a bump on a log waiting for him to get off her, smoke a Pall Mall and promise a few bucks when he got paid next week. Shower, dress and take his skinny ass home.

When Bessie was down with a powerful case of dietitis she hated Sweet Meat's guts. He had one of those metabolisms (which wasn't nothing but a tapeworm in disguise) that let him eat like a pig and still weigh only 145 pounds fully dressed and soaking wet. But she was good to him since it was hard finding good exercise partners, especially these days when you had to be so discretionary.

Bessie didn't worry about Sweet Meat. Some divorced men saw

their ex-wives on the sly, but Bessie knew his wife hadn't been giving him too much before she finally left him. He'd stopped seeing that homely, simple-minded white woman as soon as she'd made the last payment on his Lincoln. Heard it broke her heart. Last seen she was hustling around like a bag lady, scrounging up cash to buy Boss Man a Park Avenue. She'd found out the hard way that once you go black, you never go back. Only woman Bessie had given a moment's thought to when it came to Sweet Meat was Lily, and she hadn't been too much of a problem.

Was once a rumor that said Sweet Meat was trying to get next to Lily. Bessie wasn't sure how low Sweet Meat would go but she believed Lily might have indulged since hell would freeze over before her old man got out of prison. So Bessie'd put a stop to that action before it got started. She knew Lily was a cradle robber, had a 44-year-old itch only jail bait could scratch. Bessie, being a few years younger and having a taste for well-seasoned men herself, introduced Lily to a 22-year-old young, dumb and full of come-and-get-it rookie who'd been standing on the corner every since that big factory shut-down. Lily had a reputation for buying what she wanted, so Bessie'd done all three of them a favor.

She wished Sweet Meat would do her a favor and hurry up about it. Told him she had business to tend to. Give him ten more minutes before she scratched a trench down each side of his back. Sweet Meat, talking like he didn't know beans from peas said, "Gawd-damn, woman, was it that good?"

Bessie told him the honest-to-goodness truth even though she was lying about it this time. Batted her false eyelashes and said, "You know it was, sweetness!"

Bessie could Meryl Streep with the best of them. She didn't know a black woman who couldn't fake it when necessary. But the chances were slim and none of getting a high-paying leading actress role in this neighborhood unless you did a Diahann Carroll or a Diana Ross. And a white man couldn't do nothing for Bessie except introduce her to a black one. Most of the sisters Bessie knew were bit players but even Best-Supporting Actresses won Oscars. And old Oscar had been a good workout until he sucked a piece of gristle down the wrong pipe and dropped stone-cold dead.

Sweet Meat lit a cigarette on his way to the bathroom. Bessie had a see-thru shower curtain and watching him lathering himself, answered her own question about why she tolerated his shit-nanigans: "Any man looking that mouth-watering deserves to be unscrupulously chewed on. Like Maxwell House says . . . good to the last drop." Bessie's juices broiled just thinking about it. But then Sweet Meat went to playing with her mind, with his sabotaging self. Got a hump in his back and started off-key singing:

"If I don't loves you, baby: grits ain't grocery, eggs ain't poultry and Mona Lisa was a man."

Leave it to Sweet Meat to start singing about food knowing good-and-damn well Bessie was trying out the new two-day-a-week fasting diet. Breakfast food was one of her downfalls. Three jumbo eggs — one with a double yoke if she got lucky — sprinkled with salt, pepper and paprika, wisked with milk and scrambled just a tease. Bacon still wearing its rind. Flaky buttermilk biscuits sucking up to some thick brown turkey gravy, swirled around the plate till there wasn't nothing left but the pattern.

Bessie staggered to the bathroom, intoxicated by the thought of skillets sizzling and the steaming smell of Sweet Meat, and threw up a powerful stream of words. "Negro, please. If you don't hush your mouth, I'm gonna cut you a new asshole." Sweet Meat knew which way was up. Knew Bessie couldn't even look at food till midnight.

"Hey, sugar pie, honey bunch, ain't no need in you biting my head off cause you starving yo'self to death. If you hongry, come eat." Sweet Meat thought he was Mtume, singing, "I'll be your lolly-pop, you can lick me everywhere."

"Old sucker," Bessie thought, grabbing a nail file off the vanity and sawing at her chewed-ragged nails. Wondering if Sweet Meat'd ever seen *Psycho*, putting his life into her hands like that. Purposely trying to drive her crazy. He knew sweetness was her weakness. Give Bessie a Ho-Ho or a Twinkie or a Ding-Dong, anything with a cream filling in the middle, and . . . have mercy!

In Bessie's nightstand drawer was a pages-missing copy of *Sweet Savage Love* with vanilla cream-filling fingerprints on the pages where the famished young thing had conned the big bad wolf into ravishing her up. There weren't ever any black folks in those stories. Bessie thought it was a crying shame. She didn't know anything better in the world than moaning over deep dark chocolate. After the first time she'd got her nose opened to the taste of chocolate, it was all over but the shouting. And Bessie and Sweet Meat could get into some . . . shouting matches.

Sweet Meat yelled, "Woman, you better start getting dressed — "

"I don't better do nothing but be black and die!"

"Die-et, to hear you tell it. Didn't nobody tell you to sign up for them airy-o-bics classes. I just pay for 'em. Waste of good money, too. You know you'll up and quit in another week. Like last time when — "

"Look here, Walter — " Walter was Sweet Meat's given name. Bessie loaned it to him whenever he got on her best nerves.

"Look here my foot! Ain't no need in you getting pissed off at me — "

"Better to be pissed off than pissed on — "

"Now ain't that the truth. I ain't gonna say it but one more time. If you want me to drop you off, you better get yo' backfield in motion. And you a eeevilll old thing when you hongry. Maybe I'll creep on over and bring you a midnight snack. What about it? You gonna be hongry later on?"

"Don't you try sweet talking me, Walter. Always trying to booby-trap me into eating even when I don't want to. And don't you think for a minute I don't know why you don't want me taking this class. You figure I'll get all trimmed down and dump you like a hot potato. But I got a trick for you this time. I'm gonna lose these last twenty pounds whether you like it or not."

Sweet Meat gave it one last try. He'd be the last to admit it, but Bessie was right on time. He was afraid once she lost weight she wouldn't want him no more, completely ignoring the fact that Bessie'd always had herself a man, 199 pounds or 120 pounds. Bessie was a damn good looking woman, built like a brick-shit house. Smart as a whip, educated: street if not book. She could sling big words with the best of the white folks. Signify with the best of the black folks. Played the nut role only when it suited her best interests. Bessie was the wrong woman to tangle with when she was in a bad mood. Dieting always put her in a bad mood.

Not remembering that saying about he who fights and runs away living to fight another day, Sweet Meat tried forcing Bessie into surrendering to her hunger by singing a song older than his birthday:

"I want a big fat momma, big and round/a momma who can really go to town/500 pounds or mo'/just a big fat momma to roll/a big fat momma sho' do treat you right. I want — "

Bessie counter-attacked with, "People in hell want ice water and they got a better chance at getting it than you have of getting out of here alive if you don't leave me the fuck alone . . . till later on tonight." She never completely shut a door she'd want opened later in the evening. But when you were half mad with hunger and there was a T-bone drying off right in front of your face, well, somebody could get themselves killed.

Like that diet doctor who got offed by his woman. Newspapers got it all wrong. Bessie knew the real reason whatshername popped him didn't have nothing to do with jealousy over no love thang. Nothing wrong with that old antique ass white woman but hunger. Bessie'd seen their pictures in *People*. That woman looked absolutely starved, shriveled, like she hadn't had a full course meal in years. Him being a diet doctor, too. He should've known even old women need spice in their diets. But from the looks of him she would've croaked on off from malnutrition in another few years anyway. It was a simple case of kill or be killed.

Because men are a trip. They can look like who thought it, and why. Ugly clean to the bone. Tall, short. Thin, fat. It's men who make those teeter-totter heels, but you even seen one wear them? Hell no! Men make those living girdles that squash the life out of you, but you ever seen one wear them? Hell no!

But women. Women can Jane Fonda themselves to death and it still isn't enough. Just this morning Bessie was watching "Oprah" – Oprah was Bessie's hero; paid big bucks to chew the fat on national T.V. and didn't bite her tongue doing it, either; Oprah looked like she didn't half-step when it came to a good meal, herself – and not one woman in the audience was happy about the way she looked. Those with flat chests wanted them siliconed; those with big ones, wanted them cut down to size. Bessie had exercised with men with problems of their own, but the same men doctors (and it was always a man) who went on talk shows talking about cutting off fat, nipping and tucking and sucking out fat, have never come up with a surgery could add or take away from that.

One week Oprah'd done a show on people who didn't like fat people. "Stinky, sweaty fat people." Nobody perspired (the skinny word for sweat; even has a better ring to it) harder than Sweet Meat. Nobody in the neighborhood had a higher water bill than Bessie's. "Fat people are lazy." Bessie worked ten hours a day, twelve if she put in overtime, because she didn't have nothing better to do. One fat woman in the audience had "a pretty face," butt . . .

Damn if one of the guests wasn't a porky pig looking white man with chins keeping each other company. If Bessie had been in the audience, she would've jumped on his case, too. Unless somebody forgot to mention there were calories in the air, that man had been eating something. With his breathing up everything in sight, no wonder his "Size 8 or I'll divorce her" wife looked so starved – and embarrassed. Bessie would have beat that man within an inch of his life, talking about fat women like he hadn't ever seen a mirror. You expected that kind of foolishness from men, but Bessie felt women should stick together. Especially black women, who ought to know better than talk about people on account of looks. That's the very reason Bessie'd gone off on Kitty at the last aerobics class.

Bessie could hear Sweet Meat in the background yelling he was leaving her if she didn't start getting dressed, but she was thinking on what had gone down with Kitty. She said, "Don't you rush me! I was getting around before you and I expect I'll be getting around after you. So you can get to stepping if you can't wait until I get ready to go."

Sweet Meat sat on the bed and waited.

Bessie'd read Kitty the riot act. Kitty'd been acting like the alley cat she was, laughing at the new member, Ververly. Ververly'd come to class wearing black tights and a long black sweatshirt, trying to hide what she was trying to lose and not winning on either count. She was a big bright corn-fed girl, married to a good looking chocolate man who'd seen to it that Ververly was well fed every since their honeymoon: midnight snacks included from the looks of things. And Kitty was jealous. She couldn't lap it up in luxury anymore. Her husband woke up to Kitty one morning, saw the woman she had become and found himself a bigger place to lay his head. She needed a big woman to take it out on and Ververly was available.

Kitty said, "Some people just let themselves go. They don't care how they look when they go out in public. It's just a total lack of self-respect."

You'd have to be blind in one eye and couldn't see out the other not to know Kitty was signifying on Ververly who just stood in the middle of the gym grinning like she didn't know what else to do with her face, ready to cry. She'd told Bessie before class started that she'd tried everything: rotating diets, shrinking-in-the-bath-tub diets, wrapping yourself in Saran Wrap diets. Grapefruit diets. Bohemian diets. Seven day diets. Liquid diets. Lose 30 pounds in 10 day diets. Low calorie diets. High fiber diets. Diet pills that almost killed you diets. And was giving serious consideration to either locking her jaws or stapling her stomach.

Bessie understood how Ververly felt. She'd been on the diet-of-the-week routine herself. But she also understood that it was hunger making Kitty so mean and evil. Bad enough Kitty was missing breakfast, lunch and dinner, but when you were missing between meal snacks, too, somebody had to suffer. But right is right and Kitty was wrong to pick on Ververly. She was being so nasty that Bessie told her, "And some people need to go screw themselves."

"Oh, I wasn't referring to you, Bessie — "

"That's mighty white of you, Kitty." Bessie hated it when Kitty purred her words, playing big-shot proper. Dragging them out her mouth like they had enough sense to keep to themselves but Kitty wouldn't let them. So in her best Oscar-winning performance Bessie said, "I know you weren't referrrring to me. You were referrrring to Ververly. And whateverrrr extrrrra she got, least she come by it naturrrrally. Didn't go out and buy it."

Kitty's back arched, sensing an attack coming. Thought a minute about baring her claws; thought better. Tried to slink her way past it, saying, "Now, Bessie, there's no reason to get ugly — "

"Kitty, you better watch your mouth before I slap whatever taste you got left in it, out. And I know you're not trying to call me ugly, are you? Buying your best not to be ugly, aren't you? What did you and your bad boy Michael do, hit a two-for-one surgery special? Pruned your nose and you been talking through it ever since . . . when it isn't running. Capped your teeth. Silly-puttied your titties. Got yourself a 100% human hair weave and dyed that. Anything on your body an original part?

"And which bleach are you using on your face now: Ambi, Flori Roberts or Venus de Milo? Better quit using that mess. Get some Noxema or Witch Hazel and leave it at that before you fade clean away. Honey, even Clorox don't get all the dirt out."

There was nothing Kitty could say. She'd come to class from the skin doctor's office and he'd told her the same thing: she was breaking out from using all those strong chemicals on her face. Bessie wasn't one to go against somebody with degrees and awards and certificates hanging on their walls. But she didn't take as gospel everything that came out of a doctor's mouth, either. Especially a man doctor when he was talking about women's problems. He may have been acquainted with skin, but Bessie knew Kitty. Half of those bumps were boogie's. Came from a lack of meat.

Kitty should have made a dinner reservation at Chuck's wife's funeral. This neighborhood wasn't exactly known for its supply of fresh meat. A lot of hungry women were out there waiting in the cut. Bessie was glad times weren't that rough for her. Glad she had squirrel sense and always kept some nuts stored up for future emergencies.

Kitty could have handled Ververly with no problem, but Bessie was too tough, so she turned tail and went home early. Ververly thanked Bessie who then proceeded to get on Ververly's case. Said, "Honey, you're young, but you ain't never too young to learn to stand up for yourself. You've got what Kitty wants but she don't need you knowing it. The only way people like Kitty make themselves feel better is by making you think something's wrong with you.

"Look at Kitty. No bigger than a snap of the fingers, but is she happy? Sometimes all skinny means is you don't have nothing left to blame but yourself when you're not happy. Long as I have my health, my job, a roof over my head and can eat when I want to – and not necessarily in that order – I'm happy. Don't nobody pick no tree for me to shit under and that includes deciding how I should look. Any man, or woman either for that matter, don't like how I look, they know where the door is. Because nobody will ever love me like I love me. Don't you ever let nobody try to tell you about you."

And that was the end of that.

Sweet Meat had been out the shower and was seating on the bed looking like an ashy raisin. He couldn't stand Bessie's day-dreaming any longer. Asked her again, "Woman, are you going to airy-o-bics or ain't you? What the hell you been setting there thinking on all this time anyways?"

Bessie got this deliciously wicked look on her face and said, "Cutting class tonight."

Sweet Meat was always ready to rise to the occasion. "You hongry?"

"Thought you were in such a hurry?"

"Damn shame the car won't start."

"Isn't it though?" said Bessie, walking into the bathroom. She ran hot water into the tub.

After marinating in baby oil and basting herself with splashes of the new Chanel No. 5, Bessie and Sweet Meat ate dessert. Sweet Meat said, "Thank the Lawd and bless the cook." Bessie said, "My parents say you're welcome."

And the moral of the story is this: Smart men do make passes at good looking women with fat asses.

Last Summer

"How I Spent My Summer Vacation" by Diana Lancaster

THIS WAS THE best summer of my life because I spent my vacation doing a lot of fun stuff with Sharon Thompson. Sherry-Berry — people always call me Diana-Banana — got to play outside more than she had any other summer. She got to get mud on her white shorts and sand in her hair without getting a whipping or yelled at or anything. We got to stay up late and watch old Bette Davis movies on TV. We even got to go to Riverview on the bus with Tony and Jimmy Jackson and Jimmy Wilson.

On the last day of school we stayed up all night . . . well, almost all night. Berry called me on the phone and said, "My momma said to ask your momma if you can sleep over. My momma said she'll make us some popcorn and we can stay up until one o'clock in the morning and watch *Whatever Happened to Baby Jane*. So ask your momma, 'kay? Right now!"

"You sure?" I said, because Berry's momma always made her go to bed "with the chickens."

"Yep, I'm sure. You don't have to believe me if you don't want to. Just ask your momma. Wait a minute, my momma said put your momma on the phone."

After I told Berry 'kay, I yelled, "Momma, momma. Berry's

momma wants to ask you can I spend the night and stay up late and watch TV and eat popcorn. Can I?"

Momma screamed, "What did I tell you about yelling in the house," as she snatched the phone outta my hand. Then she started talking to Berry's momma. "Barbara, Diana says — "

They stayed on the phone forever. Momma got this kinda funny look on her face while she was talking to Mrs. Thompson, like she was hearing something that didn't sound too good. After she wiped some dirt outta her eyes, momma said, "Of course Diana can spend the night. She's jerking on my sleeve, so I'll put her back on the phone with Sharon while I pack her clothes. If you need anything — "

"I didn't think they'd ever get off the phone," I said.

"Bring your dolls, too, 'kay, Banana?"

"'kay. Hey, how come your momma's letting us stay up all night?"

"'cause it's summer."

"It's summer every summer and she don't let you stay up late. So why come we can stay up tonight?"

"Who cares why? Let's just do it."

Berry was always quiet and ladylike, and she was the most beautifuliest girl I had ever seen. She had good hair that was so black it almost looked blue sometimes: she wore it in pigtails like Dorothy in *The Wizard of Oz*. I have short kinky hair that never gets as straight as hers, even when momma presses it with the straightening comb. Berry had pop-eyes; my eyes are smaller and more slanted, and maybe that's why I see things more crooked than she did even though we both wore glasses. Berry had a tiny mouth like Cupid's; my mouth is wider and fuller, and I get more use outta mine than she did outta hers.

Berry almost always wore frilly dresses with puffed sleeves and even when she didn't it seemed like everything she owned was as pale as she was: all those white shorts and pastel blouses with matching socks. I like clothes you can get dirty in: blue jeans and T-shirts. I only wear dresses on Sundays.

"Hey, Sherry-Berry," Jimmy Wilson would shout. "You wanna play kickball? What'sa matter, scared to get dirty?"

I don't like Jimmy Wilson too much.

"Leave her 'lone, man," Jimmy Jackson would yell back at Jimmy Wilson. "You know she can't play kickball today. She can't get dirty 'cause she has to go to the doctor later on."

I like Jimmy Jackson.

That dumb old Jimmy Wilson would yell back at Jimmy Jackson, "She's always going to the doctor."

I screamed at him, "You'll be going to the doctor, too, if you don't leave her alone."

"Aw, Diana-Banana, why don't you split!"

I guess Jimmy Wilson thought that was funny 'cause he started laughing like a hyena, so the only thing I could do was kick him in the you-know-where. After that Tony Smith said, "You wanna play on my team?"

I like Tony Smith, too. A whole lot.

Berry would say, "Banana, you know you're not supposed to fight boys," but she laughed when she said it. We were best friends and best friends kick Jimmy Wilson when he's picking on people.

Oh well, that's how me and Berry were. On the last day of school when I spent the night, we played with our Barbies and Kens for awhile, then put on our pajamas. We always undressed together, snapping each other with our training bras.

"Banana?"

"Yep, Berry?" I said.

"Let's go to Riverview this summer."

"I go to Riverview every summer and you know it. Me and Jimmy Jackson and that dumb old Jimmy Wilson — and Tony." Saying Tony's name made me giggle.

"I know you all go. You like Tony, don't you? You like him better than you do me? I want to go to Riverview with you all this summer."

"Yep," I said, "I like Tony. No, I don't like anybody better than I like you: you're my best friend. But you know you can't go to Riverview."

"Why not?"

"Berry, quit acting so dumb. You know your momma don't let you go to no Riverview. I've been going all my life and you're eleven years old and ain't never been."

Berry pouted. "You're eleven, too. Momma said I can do whatever I want this summer, so I want to go to Riverview. So . . ."

"So, what?" I said.

"So, I'm going to Riverview. So there."

"Sure you are." I didn't believe her or her momma, about Berry could play outside and go to Riverview if she wanted to, but the movie was coming on and I wanted to see Bette Davis feed Joan Crawford a dead rat for "din-din" so all I said was, "'kay, you're going."

Fooled me! Next week Berry did too get to play outside. She ran a little slower than the rest of us, and got tired easier, but after all she was new at this. Berry was a clumsy kicker, but she could catch real good. When we played double-dutch Berry had to stand in the ropes like the boys did, instead of running in like us girls did. She was double-handed and got tangled up a lot, but even I got tangled up, sometimes, playing "Head-and-Shoulders."

I cracked up when Jimmy Wilson tried to teach her how to play mumbletypeg. I don't think Jimmy Jackson liked that too much either 'cause I knew he liked Berry, but then he should've taught her how to play himself. Jimmy Wilson would put his arm around Berry and show her how to throw the knife. You should've seen Jimmy Jackson's face.

I have to give Berry credit though, she didn't even cry when she got sand in her hair and mouth after we stomped the knife down in the sandpile and she had three tries to pull it out with her teeth when she lost the game. That night Berry took home as much of that sandpile in her P.F. Flyers as we did. I was so proud of her!

Then three weeks later, Berry went to Riverview with us the day it opened. And the way she acted, you would've thought she hadn't ever been anywhere, ever, in her whole life.

"Do I look okay?"

I told her, "We're just going to Riverview."

"Yep, but I've never been before."

"And if you don't hurry up, you won't be going now. The bus'll be coming in a few minutes and we gotta stop and get the boys." I tugged at her pigtails and then my momma started in.

"Did you put your money up?"

"Yep, momma."

"What did I tell you about saying 'Yep'? Do you have your token for the bus?"

"Ye . . . yes, momma."

"Don't eat till you're sick."

"Yes, momma."

"Don't ride the roller coaster."

"Yes, momma."

We rode the Comet every year and momma knew it. I think she just wanted to make Berry's momma feel better. I grabbed Berry's hand and snatched her to the front door after telllling my momma, "I know, don't talk to strangers on the bus."

We made a run for it and met the boys down on the corner.

"Took you two long enuff," Tony said. "You almost made us miss the bus."

"Aw, shut up!" I said. "We got here, didn't we? My momma — "

It was an A-and-B conversation but Jimmy Wilson just had to see his way into it. He said, "Yeah, I know your momma. She — "

Well, can't nobody talk about my momma but me so I said, "Get off my momma, chump. Your momma — "

"Will you two cut it out?" Jimmy Jackson yelled.

I don't know what his problem was, he was holding Berry's hand. Tony grabbed my hand and we all got on the bus and took up as much room as we could on the back seat. Berry sat by the window and you would've thought Jimmy Jackson was glued to her. Poor Jimmy Wilson didn't have no girlfriend, so he sat in the middle of the seat by himself.

I looked across Tony's shoulders at Berry and she smiled back at me. She was going to Riverview. As much as I liked Tony, and she liked Jimmy Jackson, I knew we were both wishing we had gone by ourselves this first time.

At the front entrance to Riverview, Berry just stood there and whispered in my ear, "It's bigger than the Plaza."

Our parents shopped at the Plaza, and I guess that was the biggest place Berry had ever been. The boys paid our way in while I pointed up at a flashing band of color in the sky and screamed, "That's the Comet."

"You don't really ride that thing, do you?"

"Sure, but you don't have to if you don't want to. I'll stay with you and watch the boys ride if you want me to."

"No, Banana. I want to see you flying up there. Ride it for both of us, 'kay?"

"'kay, if you're sure. I don't mind sitting with you though."

"No. I have to see you ride it this year. Ride it for me, pul-eeze."

"'kay. Let's walk around first, though."

The five of us walked around the park and Berry looked at

everything like she was trying to memorize it. We walked real slow so she wouldn't get tired. She wanted to see and do everything.

I know Riverview. I know where all the corn dog and cotton candy and snow cone stands are, where all the games and rides are, and even where the bathrooms are. But exploring the park with Berry made me feel like I had never really been to there before.

"Banana, this cotton candy melts as soon as you bite it and tickles sliding down my throat."

I kinda got mad when Jimmy Jackson licked a piece of pink off the side of her face. Jimmy Wilson didn't look too happy about it either.

I told Berry, "Don't eat too much of that stuff; it'll make your stomach hurt and we still have to eat snow cones and corn dogs."

I felt better after Tony licked a piece of blue off my nose.

We all laughed when Berry bit into her corn dog and mustard rolled down her chin and plopped on her T-shirt. Tony said, "Your momma's gonna kill you."

I licked mustard off the corner of his mouth and said, "Who cares, right, Berry. We'd die happy, right?"

For a second I thought I saw a strange look on Berry's face. I guess the sun was in my eyes wrong or something. Berry just smiled and said, "Right."

We all walked down to the Midway and Tony won me a teddy bear by knocking over some milk bottles. Jimmy Jackson won Berry a doll by shooting some ducks dead. I won Jimmy Wilson a back-scratcher at the ring toss booth since he didn't have no girlfriend to win something for, and he had looked so sad when me and Tony, and Berry and Jimmy Jackson rode through the "Tunnel of Love."

Berry got dizzy on the "Round-Up" so we decided she better not ride anymore. But she insisted on going on the ferris wheel. I rode on the seat with her and when we got stopped at the top, I asked her how she was doing.

"Fine."

"You getting dizzy yet?"

"No, I'm okay."

"You're an 'okay' lie. You look like you're about ready to pass out. We'll be down in a minute."

"I told you I'm okay. Really, Banana. You know what?"

"What?"

"That cloud over there looks just like an angel. Looks like we should just be able to reach out and touch it. Heaven looks so close up here."

"Heaven?"

"Yep, heaven. Do you ever think about heaven, Banana?"

"Not unless I'm at church, I don't. Why, do you?"

"Sometimes."

"Why?"

Berry didn't seem real sometimes. Here we were at Riverview with our boyfriends — and Jimmy Wilson — and here she was talking about clouds that looked like angels, and heaven and stuff. It just didn't make no sense.

"I don't know why," she said.

As soon as we got back to earth I pulled Tony over and told him, "We better hurry up and ride the Comet. I think Berry's getting tired."

"Did she say so?"

Much as I liked Tony, he sure could be dumb sometimes.

"No," I said, "but I think she is anyway."

"'kay. Let's go, baby."

Tony could be dumb but I liked it when he called me baby. We found a bench for Berry to sit on while we rode the Comet. And as we zoomed through the air flashing sparkles behind us, I thought I heard Berry's screams mixed up in ours.

Berry didn't go back to Riverview with us the second, third, or fourth time we went, but she still played her butt off. She learned that the sting of a crab apple fight wore off after fifteen minutes. Jimmy Jackson showed her how to blow bubble-gum bubbles and make chains with the wrappers. Berry could find all our secret bushes when she was "It" when we played "Hide-and-Go-Seek." Sometimes she would just stand next to me with her pigtails unraveling and her blouse creeping out of her dirty white shorts and say, "It sure is fun being a kid sometimes."

And I'd say, "Yep." Because it sure was.

August is a sad kind of month: Riverview closes down in August. Summer vacation is almost over; school starts in four weeks. You could still play outside after 3:30, but it's not the same as being able to play outside all day. And it's hard to talk your momma into sleepovers once school starts. So after momma finished dragging me around the Plaza buying me yucky school clothes, I asked her if Berry could spend the night. She hadn't been around much lately — doctor's appointments and stuff. I wanted to talk to her.

Berry wanted to talk, too. That night after we ate dinner, Berry and I went into my bedroom, locked the door and got into our pajamas. First thing she said was, "Have you ever kissed a boy yet?"

I stared at her. "Pul-eeze. Did you?"

"Pul — eeze. Jimmy wanted to and — "

"Wilson or Jackson?" I knew which one, but it was fun to watch her blush.

"You know good and well which one, Banana. Jackson."

"Old metal mouth? You'll cut your lip on that sharp stuff. You know good and well Jimmy Jackson just got braces. How you gonna tell your momma how you cut your lip?"

Berry didn't want to laugh, but she knew it was funny. "I'm not going to kiss his braces, Banana," she said, trying to look serious and stop shaking, all at the same time. "They don't get in the way when — "

"How do you know they won't get in the way?"

"I just know, that's how."

I was thinking to myself, "'kay, you just know how," but all I said was, "Sure, Berry. Then you can't French kiss the way they do in the movies. You gotta keep your mouth open, and he'll cut your tongue. And what about your glasses?"

"What about my glasses?"

"How you gonna kiss with glasses on?"

"You wear glasses, too. How you gonna kiss — "

"Yep," I jumped in, "but I can see without mine. Black as he is, you couldn't even find Jimmy Jackson without yours! So how you gonna kiss him?"

Berry skipped over the black part and told me how.

"Well, I'm taller than he is, so when I bend over to get to his — "

Up until then I thought maybe she had already kissed Jimmy Jackson and was just trying to find a way to tell me about it. But when she started talking this dumb stuff about bending over, I knew she hadn't.

"Dummy. You can't kiss standing up. You have to kiss sitting on the couch and then you'll be the same size. Don't you know anything at all?"

Berry couldn't think of anything smart to say back, so she said,

"I know Jimmy wants to kiss me and he doesn't want to kiss you, na, na, na . . . na, na." That was fine with me because she knew I liked Tony, anyways.

"So. I don't want to kiss him either. Tony and I already kissed."

Berry called me a liar.

"I'm not lying," I said. "He did it when we were all playing 'Truth-or-Consequences.' Tony picked consequences, so Bo-Bo made him kiss me. Na! You can ask Bo-Bo." Luckily Bo-Bo had moved last week and I knew Berry would never ask Tony about it. She might ask Jimmy Jackson, but I didn't think so.

Berry said, "Well. So — "

"Well, so what?"

"Well, so, what did it feel like?"

Uh-oh, I thought. "Well, it felt, uh, kinda good: sloppy like."

"You mean he busts slob and — "

"Dummy, I told you it's called French-kissing now. You sure can be dumb sometimes."

I felt real bad. I knew Berry hated to be called dumb and besides, I had just started calling it French-kissing myself — about two weeks ago. Berry looked like she was trying not to cry and that made me feel even worse. Momma always said I had a big mouth and that one of these days I was going to talk myself into something I couldn't get out of.

"S . . . so."

"Don't cry, Berry. I'm sorry. I didn't mean you were dumb. Come on, I'm sorry. 'kay?"

"'k . . . k . . . kay. How are you supposed to kiss a boy when you got glasses on?"

Momma was right — as usual. I'd talked myself into this mess. So I said, "Wipe your eyes first and I'll tell you. Wipe your eyes first though."

"'kay. Tell me now?" Berry was sure a fast wiper.

"Got your Barbie?" I'm a fast thinker.

"Yep."

"'kay. Now here's Ken. Stick Barbie's arms out — "

"Like this?" Berry sure wasn't making this easy.

"Yep. Now — "

"Wait a minute," Berry said. "Their legs are all twisted up. My momma would beat my butt — "

"Your momma ain't gonna be there, dum . . . Berry."

"Banana, you know my momma is always there."

"That's true, mine, too. 'kay, but look, your legs ain't gonna be like this 'cause Barbie and Ken's legs only bend straight out. So just pretend, will you?"

"Pretend what?"

"Pretend their legs can bend at the knees. Then their feet will be on the floor."

We were both really getting into this now. We were getting so carried away I think Berry was convinced I really had kissed Tony.

"Then how is Ken gonna get his arms around Barbie?"

"Well, I don't know; let's see. If you put this arm here and that arm there, and — "

"And this isn't gonna work either."

"Yep?"

"Yep!"

Berry was right, but I worked my way outta it. "Well?"

"Well, what?"

"Well," I said, "I gotta idea."

"Uh-oh. Well, what is it?"

"You'll think it's weird," I said.

"All of your ideas are weird."

"Yep, but you like them."

"Yep, usually. Come on, tell me. Pul-eeze."

"'kay. We could always practice."

"Practice what?"

"Kissing, dummy." That one slipped. Berry missed it.

"When?"

"Now."

"Where?"

"Here."

"With who?"

"With us."

"Who we gonna kiss?"

"Who do you think?"

And then Berry caught on. And I knew I wanted this to happen as much as I had wanted to go to Riverview with Berry alone, her first time out. It's too hard to explain, but somehow I knew Berry didn't want us to stop now any more than I did. We had to do it.

"Oh? Oooh! I get you now. Can we do that? I mean isn't it — "

I didn't want us to have too much time to think about it so I said, "We dress in front of each other when we go swimming, right?"

"Yep."

"And we sleep in the same bed when you stay over, don't we?"

"Yep."

"Hey. Remember that time when we were real little and we both tried to pee standing up over the toilet?"

"Yep. That was funny. I told you you had weird ideas."

"I got more in than you did."

"Yep, and my momma whipped our butts. I told you she's always there."

"Yep. But I heard your momma and my momma laughing about it over the phone."

"We couldn't understand how boys did it then." We both laughed.

"We understand how they do it now, though, don't we?" We both laughed again.

When she stopped laughing, Berry said, "Yep."

"That's why I think we should practice. You don't wanna look dumb when you kiss Jimmy Jackson, do you?"

"No. I guess not."

"Well, come on then. We're best friends."

"We're blood sisters."

"That's even better. So you wanna try it?" I knew she did or Berry would have stopped us a long time ago. We just had to feel each other out a little more first.

"If you want to."

"You sure?" I said.

"I'm sure, if you're sure."

"'kay, but we gotta put my dolls up first, 'kay?"

We threw Barbie and Ken on my dresser and jumped on the bed. Berry got in a hurry all of a sudden.

"'kay, now what do we do first? Want me to take my glasses off?"

"Nope. We both wear 'em so we may as well leave 'em on so we can see what we're doing."

Berry said, "I thought you were supposed to kiss with your eyes closed."

"You do after you know what you're doing. You wanna be the boy first or the girl first?"

"What dif does it make?"

"It's kinda hard to explain. You just had to be there when Tony kissed me."

I wanted to stop lying and tell Berry that Tony hadn't kissed me, but it didn't seem fair to her to stop now. So I kept it up.

"Where were you Wednesday? We played 'Truth-or-Consequences' and everything."

Berry always looked sad when she said she had gone to the doctor. I'd look sad, too, if I had to go to the doctor as much as she did. Berry looked even sadder when she said, "You always do the good stuff when I'm not around."

"Well, you're here now, so come on. You gonna be the boy or the girl?"

"I just asked you, what dif does it make?"

"And I just told you, you had to be there. 'kay, look, I'll be Tony — since you don't see it — and you'll be me. Roll over so you can be on my right side."

"But I'm right-handed."

"So, it doesn't matter; I was, too. Then Tony put his right arm around my shoulder; like this. Then he put his left hand on my waist: like this. Now turn left into me."

"'kay. Then I can put my arms around you like this. Right?"

"Yep. I thought you didn't know how to do this?"

"I don't. Go 'head."

"'kay, you don't! Now watch it 'cause our glasses are gonna bump. Lean your head to the right."

"Like this?"

"Yep. Now kinda open your mouth a little."

Berry almost pulled back, then. "Why?"

"Well, Tony kinda licked my tongue and I liked that."

"You're so-o ba-a-ad."

"But I liked it."

Berry giggled. "I bet you did."

I laughed. "Shut-up and kiss me."

"'kay."

So we kissed. I didn't mean to, but I went "Uhmm" while we did it.

"Uhmm? What's 'uhmm' for?"

"I'm not real for sure, but boys always seem to moan when they kiss."

"Why?"

Berry never ran out of questions, so I had to keep coming up with answers.

"I guess it feels good to them."

"It feels good to me . . .uh . . .to girls, too, I mean. So can't we moan, too?"

"Yep. Did it really feel good to you?"

"Yep, kinda salty. You really have soft lips."

"You do, too. I think all girls do. That's that popcorn salt."

I was really glad when Berry asked, "Can I be the boy now?" because I wanted to kiss her again, too.

"You really want to do it again?" I said, just to be sure.

"Uh-huh. Can we take our glasses off now?"

"Remember what you saw?"

"Yep, but my eyes cross up when I look at something that close up. Makes we wanna laugh. So we'll take our glasses off, 'kay?"

"'kay."

"Uhmm."

"Uhmm."

Berry said, "It works better without glasses, doesn't it?"

"Yep," I said. "You feel kinda hot?"

"And tingly?"

"Like drinking hot chocolate after falling down ice skating."

"Yep," Berry said. "Can I stay in your arms for awhile?"

"Yep, like we do when we watch *The Birds* and stuff like that."

"You think boys ever do stuff like this?"

"I don't think so."

Berry said, "Why don't they? It's so — "

"'cause they're dumb." But I knew what Berry really meant. It was so . . . I don't know . . . just so . . . something.

"We start school in a couple of weeks." Berry started looking sad again and said, "So I guess we won't be able to do this kind of stuff anymore."

"No, I guess not. Why won't we?"

I wished Berry would look happy again. I didn't like to see her look that way, like she was just giving up on something. But all she said was, "I don't know why. It just seems to work out that way sometimes."

I didn't know what "it" was, but whatever it was, I didn't like "it."

It made Berry too sad. I told her, "I don't want things to work out that way. I want us to be best friends forever."

"And have your weird ideas keep getting us into trouble?"

"Yep. Sometimes I'm not sure I want to grow up, Berry."

"Me either, Banana. Hug me tighter."

"'kay. D . . . don . . . don't cry."

"Y . . . yo . . . you're crying, too."

"What's wrong with us?" I said.

"I . . . I . . . I don't know either."

"Berry?"

"Yep, Banana?"

"I love you." I don't know what made me say that, but whatever it was, it made Berry say it, too.

"I love you, too, Banana."

"Always?"

Berry said, "Always and forever."

"Cross your heart and hope to die?"

"Cross my heart and hope to die."

"Berry, let's not ever get too old — "

"To lay in each other's arms and cry?"

"Yep."

Berry whispered, "'kay," and then we fell asleep.

Berry was in the hospital on the first day of school. At first I was glad because if she had to get sick, at least she had waited until school started and not missed our summer vacation. But a week later Berry died of something I tried to look up in the dictionary the night after momma snuck me into the hospital. Berry had tubes stuck all over her that were connected to a machine behind her bed. The machine drew zig-zaggy lines on some paper and it kept on going beep . . . beep . . . beep. But the worst part was the brown crusty tube taped to her mouth.

I went to Berry's wake, but I didn't go to the funeral 'cause the undertaker put too much of that stuff in her that they put in you when they take all your blood out. That stuff made Berry's face look too fat and I didn't like seeing her look like that.

I was real sad when Berry died, real real sad. Because I knew that I would really kiss Tony one day, but the only boy Berry had ever kissed was me, and that just wasn't fair.

And that is how I spent my summer vacation.

Heaven vs. Hell

I SAY THE FIGHT started in Heaven although my niece, Dee, insists it started in Hell. At the time she was in the kitchen slapping Pillsbury's Ready to Spread Frosting on a store-bought angel food cake – Dee couldn't cook from scratch to save her life – and I was at the basement stove adding cayenne pepper, eight dashes of tobasco, two cloves of garlic and jalapeno peppers to the double broiler, so we had different perspectives on the situation. But we agreed that around 2:00 a.m. all heaven broke loose in Hell.

I hadn't thrown a Heaven-and-Hell party in two years. But it was only October and people were already talking that "You having another New Year's party, Emma?" smack. Figured it being Halloween, why not kill two birds with one stone? I wouldn't have to spend all that money right after Christmas, and if Dee would collect the cut in Heaven, I could call a tonk game at the same time and raise my November, and maybe December house note. Play $5 and $10, $5 on high card, and could probably do some of my Christmas shopping, too. Promised Dee I'd give her the money to play since she didn't gamble any better than she could cook.

Halloween is a good time to party, you can break all the rules. Be whoever you want, or really are. Wear a disguise, or drop one.

Demand to be treated well, or retaliate if you aren't. Instant gratification . . . or else. You don't even have to think up a theme or set a mood since the season decorates itself: the moon is usually full, the night is damp. But you have to watch out for that old man in the moon, especially when he's fully inflated, because sometimes he plays a few tricks of his own, with your mind.

Saturday afternoon Dee and I dusted the furniture, set up the card tables, opened a new carton of cards, laid out coasters, broke down and set out my expensive, heavy crystal ashtrays. Taped a blue and white Heaven sign on the dining room door, a red and black Hell one on the basement door. Started simmering the chili, cranked up the ice cream maker. Restocked the up and downstairs' bars. Saturday night Dee and I were ready for anything except what happened after Tiny beat the shit out of Moe.

I don't know what got into Tiny . . . wait a minute, I take that particular lie back. I do know. Just didn't think she'd ever do anything about Moe because Tiny was as desperate as most of these women I know. Desperate with a capital D.

Dee's desperate. Thirty-four years old, cute as all get-out with those Chinamen eyes, curly hair, dimples; about a size 12; smart when it comes to working with numbers, which is why I like her to cut my games. But she was definitely standing in the wrong line when they passed out the sense you need in dealing with men.

Dee works every day so every weekend she can take her old man, Bobby, out on the town. Bobby. Bobby Shorter! Black as the edge of night, knock-kneed, slew-footed, greasy hair all roached back, foosty/funky/foul-mouthed, ain't worked a day in his life and ain't likely to, Bobby. Likes to duke Dee up from time to time. I've offered to blow him away the next time he beats her up. After all, family is family; Dee calls me Aunt Emma even though she's only one of Uncle Eddie's daddy's sister's people. I've always liked the child, trying my best to keep her alive. But she had a spell when I even mentioned hurting "her" Bobby.

"Oh God, Aunt Emma, no," she said. "Please don't hurt my Bobby. He didn't mean it. He . . ."

"Didn't mean it? The hell you preach. What do you mean he didn't mean it? What did you do, ask him to give you a black eye?"

Dee started whining like a crumb-snatcher, made me want to pop her one, myself. "Bobby doesn't mean to hurt me. He's just frustrated because he can't find a decent paying job. And I didn't make it any better. I came home from work and started nagging him about not starting dinner . . . "

"Nagging him? That sorry son-of-a-bitch not only should have had dinner ready, but had your bath water hot and carried you to the tub. Nagging him. I'd do more than nag him . . ."

"Bobby says that's the whole problem between black men and women now. That we're trying to emasculate them. Bobby says it's always been easier for a black woman to find a job and we throw it up in their faces. Bobby says black women need to stand behind their men and build them up instead of trying to tear them down all the time."

"Uh-huh. I'd build him up all right. Build him up a casket and drop him six feet. And will you please explain to me what any of that shit has to do with Bobby hitting you because he was too lazy to get up off his good-for-nothing ass and cook dinner. If all you want is somebody to cook, and Bobby won't even do that, get rid of him and find yourself a good wife."

"Aunt Emma — " Dee said, in that voice she uses when I've hit too close to home, " — Bobby isn't lazy. He'd been job hunting all day and I guess he had too many beers when he got home. We just got into a silly little argument — I apologized for — "

"You apolo . . . save it, Dee." I knew the child wasn't wrapped too tight, but I didn't realize she had completely unraveled. Bobby had caused more brain damage than I suspected. I didn't have the stomach for any more "Bobby says" because it was just the same old psychological bullshit men always use when running down their inventory of reasons to beat up on women, usually followed by "I'm sorry, baby, it'll never happen again." My ex-husband tried to play those mind games with me one time . . . and one time only.

I remember I was rushing around one morning like a chicken with his head cut off, trying to get dressed for work and cook breakfast at the same time. My ex started bitching. I knew he wasn't really upset over breakfast. His unemployment was getting ready to run out and he still hadn't found a job, so I was trying to be nice. I suggested, just suggested mind you, that maybe he should take any type of job until he could find something in his line. Hell, I've had quite a few jobs I didn't want in my lifetime, but when you're unemployed, any job is better than no job.

No sooner had I got the words out — whopp — he popped me smack in the middle of my mouth. I fell backwards against the stove. They say your whole life flashes in front of your eyes? I wasn't dying but I thought to myself, "Ain't this about a blip. No man, including my father, ever hit me and I'm going to stand here and let this bastard get away with it?" So I prayed, "Lord, give me strength and a good aim," and threw that pot of grits dead in his face. He had first, second, and third degree burns. His new wife ought to be down on her knees thanking me every day of her life because I hear he not only worships the ground she walks on, but works a full and part-time job.

I haven't sworn off men but my mama didn't raise no fool, either. She told me, "Emma, you can stop a man from beating on you. The police don't give a damn. Once they leave, if they ever show up, he'll only kick your ass harder for calling them in the first place. Cause it ain't nothing but a power play. A man who'll beat his woman and children will knock you down getting out of the way if he had to fight a man. So you fight him like a man because if you let him get away with it one time, he'll do it again. You're gonna feel pain whether you stand there and take it or fight back. Hurt is hurt. But at least make him know he's been in a battle. I guarantee you he won't make that mistake more than one time." And either my daddy was born wih good sense or mama had a mean right hook because I never heard him raise his voice, to say nothing of raising anything else. Good training begins at home.

But Dee isn't the only woman I know who is brain-damaged when it comes to men. Half of the wives coming to my party weren't any better. Dee was still a child but women my age, in their late forties, early fifties, ought to know better. I keep preaching, telling them to let those no-account scrubs go, but they keep hanging in for the whole fifteen rounds. Then come to me with their sob stories. I don't know why they ask me for advice. What I say goes in one ear, and their husbands knock it out the other. Ann Landers could write Dear Abby, and neither one of them could figure out what to do with these women.

Now where was I? You have to excuse me because I tend to go off just thinking about some of this shit. But it's important for you to know where I'm coming from if you're going to understand what happened in Hell.

My guests arrived in twos and fours a little after 10:30 p.m. Cookie and Clarence McGee were there first, as usual. Clarence liked to make an early appearance, and a fast gettaway, leaving Cookie to either bum a ride home or stay with me for breakfast. Cookie walked through the front door smooth-faced, slip showing and a couple of buttons in the wrong holes, so I knew she was taking Valium. Clarence must have been up to his old tricks.

Cookie called Clarence "the fugitive." When she was trying to impress the girls she said, "As long as the fugitive brings his paycheck home every week, I don't give a damn what else he does." I've seen the fugitive in action and he'd fuck a snake if you held its head down. Cookie'd cried on my shoulder the times he brought home more than a pay-check: a doctor's appointment slip for her to get two shots of penicillin and some seven day pills; two years later, a picture of a boy with Clarence's eyes, nose and mouth. Actions beat as loudly as words, and Clarence had hit Cookie with almost everything but his fists.

I smelled Jackie and Baxter — been so long since I called Baxter's first name I can't remember what it is — coming a mile off. Jackie's perfume cleared my sinuses, Baxter's after-shave just out right stank, and those matching jogging suits had to go. Talk about me and my shadow. Where Baxter led, Jackie followed. When Baxter said jump, Jackie was already three feet in the air before she asked how high. Baxter said no wife of his would ever work and none of the three of them — four including Jackie, which should have told her something — ever had. When Jackie was trying to impress the girls she said, "Baxter — " — I don't think she remembered his first name either — "says I could get a part time job, if I wanted to, but really, girls, why should I? He just got a big raise, so why should I?" I told her she should because she wanted to.

The forty, but looking ten years older, Turner twins, real names Dawn and Donetta, nicknamed Lush and Lush-ess because after five years of marriage to two of the Franklin brothers, they could drink any man under the table, arrived as clean as the Board of Health. Both wearing silk dresses, snake-skin shoes. Lush preferred Gucci, Lush-ess, Louis Vuitton. Intelligent women, both working for the State, so it must have been in the genes.

Only women whose father's name was Dirty Dog, and whose mother dressed sharper than a tack just to go to the liquor store, would marry two men called Low-Life and Swifty. Those Franklin boys were as handy with their hands as Dirty Dog Turner, speaking ill of the dead, used to be. Instead of gold chains, Lush was sporting a cervical collar. I didn't believe that fender/bender/whiplash story, but if it was a lie, it was Lush's life. Surprisingly, Lush-ess had left her dark glasses at home. The Turner twins didn't have to say anything to impress the girls because they were impressive. The worse those Franklin boys made them feel, the better Lush and Lush-ess dressed, like neglected houseplants that thrived despite sporadic waterings.

Tiny came with Moe. Moe lived with Tiny because she had a good job. Tiny lived with Moe because she was ugly. I'm not talking about Tiny, beauty is in the eye of the beholder. But Tiny had known she was ugly all her life. Her mother had told her so, her father had told her so. Her classmates were in agreement. So were the looks of strangers as she passed them on the street. And you know as well as I do that no matter what they say, men don't count personality if it isn't wrapped in a pretty cellophane package.

It's hard to pinpoint why Tiny is ugly. Like anyone else she has eyes that cry, a nose to smell trouble coming, two ears to hear the gossip and a mouth to either spread it or stop it. But things weren't arranged symmetrically on her dry, patchwork looking face: Tiny'd had exanthema when she was five and her skin never recuperated. Her left eye had a tendency to wander, especially when she was upset, so you were never really sure whether she was looking at you, through you, at the person next to you, or at herself. She broke out a lot and scarred easily, thick maroon keloid scars. Her body was a display case of cuts and bruises she'd received from childhood on. So she paid pretty men like Moe to live with her.

Moe thought he was God's gift to women. He was almost as pretty as Lush and Lush-ess, with his cinnamon-tinted soft skin, deep set eyes, long lashes, full moist lips. Broad shoulders, narrow waist, tight round ass. Egg and sperm must have fought long and hard over what to make Moe, finally copped and took the easy way out. I'd have serious problems being with a man who looked more like a woman than I did, but to each his own. With her bad eye Tiny pretended some of the admiring glances tossed Moe's way included her, she looked good because he did. With her good eye, she knew they weren't. It was her fantasy and she paid well to live it.

But at thirty-nine, Tiny was beginning to wake up and smell the bacon. She was starting to ask me those coming-to-your-right-mind questions. "Emma — " she said, "how do you live by yourself?"

"Peacefully."

"No, Emma, you know what I mean. Don't you need someone to be there for you?"

"Honey, haven't you looked around the block recently? How many men do you see who are at home for their wives? I'm not saying there aren't any good men left . . . God only knows where they are. And fifty per cent of all marriages end in marriage so somebody's doing something right, somewhere. I just haven't found a man whose company I enjoy more than my own. I'll take a cat and a good woman friend any day of the week than to put up with some of the shit you . . . Sorry, Tiny. But you know me. I get carried away."

"I wish I had your strength."

I meant it a couple of different ways when I said, "Start working out." Tiny was going to need some muscle if she remained a punching bag for Moe. With her low self-esteem, she'd need even more muscle to leave him. All I could do for her was be there when she needed me. Help her pick up the pieces one way or another. I was glad she came to the party. She'd been spending too much time away from everyone and that wasn't healthy.

A few other folks I hadn't seen in years and didn't remember inviting drifted in. And then, up walked trouble. Bobby brought up the rear with a couple of hoodlums – and a girl. Now Bobby knows I don't allow confusion in my house. And knowing me as well as he does, I didn't think, and Dee didn't appreciate, him bringing that girl to my party. I started to put them out but changed my mind, hoping her presence would bring Dee out of her Bobby-induced trance. It didn't.

Dee got mad at the girl and started talking this off-the-wall nonsense. "Look at her, Aunt Emma. Lounging over my man. I could kill her."

"For what? She hasn't done a thing to you."

Dee's conscience was trying to tell her something but she refused to listen. She said, more to herself than to me, "Makes me so mad."

I tried to help her thinking by saying, "Besides the fact that don't nothing get mad but dogs and cats, who makes you so mad?"

Dee called the girl out her name. "That . . . that slut!"

"I've been trying to tell you for years that Bobby ain't nothing but a slut."

"Don't be funny, Aunt Emma. I'm talking about that . . . that – "

"I just don't know about you, Dee. I keep drumming it into your head that you can't make anybody do something or be something just because you want them to." Talk about not taking my own advice. But it is hard when you love someone, and I love Dee like I would my own child, if I'd had any. So I went on. "You're mad at that woman but she didn't come here by herself. Bobby brought her. Because he wanted to. And quit talking that foolishnes about killing her. Bobby has all but beat your brains out but you'd rather die than talk about killing him."

Dee's desperate but she still has one of my ways: she might not always tell the truth, especially when it comes to Bobby, but she recognized it when she heard it. And she knew I was telling her right. In Dee's case though, hard heads make soft asses. All she said was, "Just drop it, Aunt Emma?" I did because Jackie was riffling the cards and I needed Dee's mind clear to collect my cut.

Most of the women played in Heaven. Fifty or sixty dollars was about all the money they were willing to lose at tonk. Even at $3 and $6, $3 on high card, I could come out ahead if they got down to serious business. But between Lush and Lush-ess mixing gin-and-sevens every half hour, Jackie talking about the non-existent job she turned down, Dee singing the black-and-Bobby blues and Cookie adding her two cents every ten minutes, it could take half the night to make any money. Most of what went on in Heaven was all talk.

Tiny and I played in Hell with the men: Money will make you grow hair on your chest. A lot of women feel intimidated gambling with men but as far as I'm concerned there's nothing to get all hot and bothered about if you keep your eyes open and your purse shut. You have to watch Bobby like a hawk, make sure he takes the top card and not pull a discard from underneath it. Clarence was lucky with aces but I was like Cookie: couldn't catch him at it, so I couldn't call him on it. I've got a trick or two of my own, so everything evens out in the long run. Nobody wins much money at tonk but the house . . . need I say more?

People were alternating between Heaven and Hell, depending on their taste buds, trying to find a happy medium between chili so spicy your nose ran, your eyes watered — and I've only got two bathrooms — and cake so rich and gooey your jaws locked. I should learn the trick of turning water into wine because I didn't get a taste of my own Chivas; folks were buying up the liquor quicker than I could pour it. But I kept the number to Yellow Cab right by the phone; I'd let people spend the night before I'd let them drive home drunk.

Dee put an old Millie Jackson cut on the stereo in Heaven. Lush and Lush-ess were swaying in their seats, moaning, "Amen, sing it, girl" while Millie sang about Low-Life and Swifty. B.B. King was doing his thing on the stereo in Hell. I knew the men were having a good time because Clarence was still drinking and gambling and usually by that time, the fugitive had hit the trail. Baxter ordered Jackie — and she came running — to get down in Hell and slow dance with him, for one record, which she did. She went back to Heaven with a smile on her face. It takes so little to make some folks happy but if she liked it I loved it

Even I cut up a small section of the rug with, believe it or not, one of Bobby's less hoodlum-looking buddies. I don't know why all young men think older women are so desperate. All my fingers work, not a bit of Arthur in them. But that little boy thought he was turning me on until I told him some things that cooled him off. Like I said, Halloween is a great time for a party.

But you should never count your chickens before they hatch. Just like Candid Camera, when you least expect it . . . Everybody was dancing and eating and drinking and losing money, and Moe had to go and act a fool. He'd been playing Houdini all night. One minute you'd see him in Heaven, flirting with some friend of Jackie's who had rung my doorbell around 1:00 a.m. asking if Jackie was there. And poof, the next minute he was back in Hell, taking Tiny's money; I had him on paper for $50 myself. It was when Tiny finally closed the bank and wouldn't give him any more cash that all hell broke loose.

Money isn't the root of all evil, the lack of it is and Moe had been drinking and losing his and then Tiny's money all evening. He was on a losing streak. After getting beat in Hell on the $5 and $10 table, he figured he could go up to Heaven and win at least some of his money back. But he couldn't even tonk out on the women.

Moe got his ass up on his shoulders and hung around in Heaven for awhile. As long as it took him to con Jackie's friend out of $30. Moe had charm. The way Tiny explained it, he had a way of making you feel you were looking in a mirror when you looked into his eyes, that his reflection was yours, or some romanticized bullshit like that. That's why Moe always went with unattractive women, they fell for that "Look into my eyes" routine. Jackie's friend was a ditz. If she had kept her money in her pocket, none of this would have happened.

Moe came back to Hell and took Clarence's seat at the card table. Since he hadn't won a hand in over an hour, naturally Tiny wanted to know where he'd gotten the money. She didn't make a scene, just bent over his shoulder and whispered, "Where did you get that money?"

Moe performed. "You didn't give it to me so don't worry about it."

Baxter laughed until Tiny's bad eye wandered in his direction. I knew why he laughed. Baxter had started enough arguments with women to be able to spot them coming a mile down the road. Arguments between men and women are so predictable because they're always the same ole, same ole. Women bring up the time "ten years ago, on the eighth of April, around 5:00 p.m., when the sun was getting ready to go down, and I was sitting on the couch, and the baby was sick, and you walked in wearing the blue shirt with a cigarette burn on the sleeve and lipstick on the collar." Women can't just drive up and honk, they have to take the scenic route to the problem and by the time they arrive, they've forgotten where they were going.

Men speed through the yellow light and run you over. First they attack the way you looked. Then they ask the question which if you knew the answer to it, you probably wouldn't be with them in the first place. The question is always the same . . . "Who do you think you are?"

Tiny started driving. "Moe, the last time we came to a card party, I didn't know until three weeks later that you owed the house money. I just don't want to leave another game owing money so if Dee gave it to you, I wish you'd just say so." Tiny knew Dee was a soft touch when it came to money; Tiny hadn't seen Jackie's friend come in.

Moe knew he had an audience, so he ran Tiny over. "What the hell did I tell your ugly ass about questioning me about my business?"

Tiny scraped her gumption off the sidewalk and said, "I'm making it my business."

Moe pushed back his chair and stood up, towering over Tiny. Later on, while he was getting stitches in his head, Moe told the emergency room doctor it was the liquor that made him knock Tiny backwards over my good card table chairs, saying, "Get your ugly ass out of my face, woman. Who the fuck do you think you are?"

I didn't start this fight but I could damn sure end it. Besides the fact that I paid good money for my furniture, I liked Tiny. I told Moe, "Obviously you were raised in a barn, but I don't stand for fighting in my house."

Moe tried to square off on me. Me! He mocked me, saying, "Since you don't stand for no fighting in your house, you can sit the fuck down, too."

He rared back his fist. I weaved out of his range and reached for the straight razor I kept taped under the card table. Both of us had forgotten about Tiny until she cold-cocked Moe upside the back of his head with my expensive, heavy crystal ashtray.

Moe was out for the count. Tiny rolled him over on his back, got down on her knees stradling his chest, and beat the cuteness off his face. Tiny didn't scratch him like a woman, she beat him like a man. There wasn't a man in Hell brave enough to attempt to break them up.

Whoop! All any woman looking into Moe's eyes for the next few days would see were reflections of what goes around, comes around. Smacko! Moe always wanted a gold tooth and Tiny gave him the perfect excuse for getting one. She didn't have the strength to beat and talk, so she just beat. But the rest of the men in Hell started shouting: "Man, you just gonna lay there and let her kick your ass like that?" Moe was in no position to let Tiny do anything. He couldn't stop her.

The door to Hell swung wide open and the women came down from Heaven to see what all the commotion was about. By the time they reached the bottom step, all they could really see was Baxter and Clarence trying to grab Tiny's arms and pull her off Moe. She kicked Baxter; she elbowed Clarence. For all of the two seconds that Tiny was off of Moe, he tried to fight back but she had anger on her side.

Maybe if Bobby hadn't said, "Ain't no way in hell I'd just lay there and let a woman beat on me. I know how to keep my woman in line"; maybe if Baxter hadn't said, "That's what happens when you let a woman go to work. She starts making a little money and forgets who's the boss"; maybe if Clarence had left the party like he usually did; maybe if the Franklin brothers hadn't started laughing and taking bets on who would win, Hell would have cooled off. I don't allow confusion in my house, but since the day that David decked Goliath, these things have to happen every once in awhile.

More than likely, it was little Tiny wailing away on Moe. But just as likely it was the memory of jaws that still hurt when the weather changed, sick days used for sprained wrists and blackened eyes, and money spent on one-sided counseling sessions that started the chain-reaction. Lush started it off.

She walked up to Low-Life, told him the sober thoughts she could only say to the girls when she was drunk, yanked that cervical collar off her neck and scratched him down the side of his face with the diamond ring she had bought to match the diamond bracelet she had bought when Low-Life punched her two months ago.

Swifty saw Lush-ess coming and said, "Don't be no fool like your sister." He asked the question that Lush-ess had finally figured out the answer to: "Who do you crazy Turner women think you are?" Lush-ess showed him by cracking that gin bottle against his skull.

Dee was a big surprise. She asked the woman Bobby had brought to the party if she wouldn't mind waiting outside, Bobby would be out in a minute. The woman told Bobby, "Later," and left him there. Bobby didn't know what to expect but he still believed he could keep his women in line. Dee walked over to the stove. I had just added cayenne pepper, eight dashes of tobasco, two garlic cloves and jalapeno peppers to the chili, and brought it back to a rolling boil. Dee's hands were sticky from slapping Pillsbury's Ready to Spread Frosting on a store-bought angel food cake. Maybe that helped tighten her grip on the pot. She carried it up to her Bobby. Bobby couldn't move so he took it like a man: he screamed.

I didn't call the police right away. After all, it was just a little domestic dispute and the police don't like to be bothered until they can take names and collect bodies. But while we were waiting for the paramedics to come and collect Moe, I couldn't help noticing how ugly those Turner twins looked, and how Tiny had turned into a swan.

The Deterioration of 47th Street

(an excerpt)

I USED TO LIVE in a palace before the rats and the roaches and the "no" peope invaded the kingdom. Before the management removed the jimmied mailboxes and installed shiny new silver ones in the front office, under heavy security. Before intercoms, buzzers, peepholes, sliding chains and two dead bolt locks replaced welcome mats and unlocked doors. Before four lettered words were sprawled across the sidewalks, covering the faint outlines of hopscotch games, and gangland battle cries – "Stone to the bone/D to the knee/Blackstone run it!" – were splashed against the bricks where balls were bounced during Off-the-Wall. Before shrieks of laughter became silent nods in passing, "Please stay off the grass" gardens shriveled, yellowed and died, and the sweet aromas floating from the basement store, Harold's Chicken Shack, Ringo's Bar-be-que and Mamie's Bakery were overpowered by the stench of drying blood, vomit on curbstones, urine in alleyways, and sex – begged or borrowed, stolen or sold.

Semblances of normalcy remained. For two years after, there were still annual Easter egg hunts, trick or treats (chewed only after parental inspection), carol singing around the illuminated Baby Jesus sleeping in the manger in the courtyard. Troop 394 still sold

Girl Scout cookies, but parents walked shotgun to collect the money. Roller skating, bike riding, and "Throw the Whip" on the swing sets. Four goldfish still swam in the rock pond in the back of the old building. And for that little while, the Rosenwald was pregnant each spring, gave birth to Eden in the summer, became the Enchanted Forest in the fall, and a Winter Wonderland from November to March.

But we no longer knew if the fireflies flashed after the sidewalk lanterns flickered at 8:00 p.m. We weren't allowed to sit on the benches, sneak a discarded cigarette butt, and search for the Big Dipper. Precautions were taken: the once unbarred entryways to the Rosenwald were now gated, clanged shut and locked, promptly at 10:00 p.m. But sometimes during the changing of the guards who patrolled the Rosenwald, and who we suspected now loaded their guns with more than one bullet, Mr. Watchman tripped over Belinda's slashed, naked body in the "Submarine."

I was born in Chicago, Illinois; the Windy City; Chi-Town; South Side. And even after what happened to Belinda, and with no apologies to all the people who lived in Hyde Park and Pill Hill, I will always say that there wasn't a better place to grow up than in the Rosenwald on 47th Street. To me, the Rosenwald was 47th Street — the best of it, and the worst of what it became.

The Rosenwald was a brick chain of buildings, linked and stretched the long blocks between 47th Street and 46th, between Wabash and Michigan, from first to fifth floor, not including the roof and the basement. If Skinner had been the architect, he could've designed a more complex layout. The rooftops were manageable: there were walkways and building address markers so you could always tell where you were; if you looked down over the ledges you could see in and outside the walls of the Rosenwald. But the basement was a disorienting maze of corridors that wound passed secluded rooms — laundry rooms, boiler rooms, storage rooms, the janitor's room — that eventually led to the "Submarine."

I don't know why we called it the "Submarine." Maybe because of the plaque that dangled from one wall, engraved in honor of someone whose name had been erased by time, but you could still make out the design on a ship carved into the wood frame. Maybe because of the little round windows that faced nothing but the damp, crumbling foundation behind them; the floor-to-ceiling metal pipe, cemented in the center of the "Submarine," that we imagined was a periscope, raised and lowered to spot approaching enemies. Who really remembers why we christened that room with that name? But the "Submarine" it was, and until management walled it in, forever sealing its mystery, dead bolting another doorway, the "Submarine" it stayed. And since it was seldom, if ever, that the older residents went down to the "Submarine," there didn't seem to be any real reason for its existence other than a room to do, and hide, secrets as we got older.

Mr. Watchman, the oldest guard at the Rosenwald, sludged his way across the roof and through the basement at regular intervals. But we knew his schedule. He tried to catch us off guard one time, but since he was so overweight, his heavy footsteps and husky wheezes were red lights and warning bells announcing his approach. And because Mr. Watchman was a tortoise, slow and predictable, all of our first sexual experiences happened in the "Submarine."

My first drop of menstrual blood dripped down my leg while waiting for Belinda to light a cigarette down in the "Submarine." I had rounded second base, Belinda third, one especially long hot summer down in the "Submarine." But not much more besides promises made, and because Mr. Watchman might one day fool us, too scared to be kept. And once the "no" people started moving in, you never knew who might have found their way through the maze and caught you.

Belinda and I knew everybody up and down 47th Street, and they knew us. They were the "yes" people; anytime we made a request, their answer was always, "Yes!" Miss Emily did our heads, and scorched our ears, "Yes!" for free if we sweated back our roots before our next weekly visit. Mr. Fuller, "Yes!" always saved us his personally scrunched and brown bagged, greasy bar-be-qued potato chips, and "Yes!" slipped us giant dill pickles with a peppermint stick stuck down the middle. Tyrone, who worked the newsstand under the 47th Street El-tracks, always ordered us, "Yes!" the latest editions of Modern Romance and True Confessions, and never told our parents that we read them. "Yes!" Mr. Blackwell taught us paino, Miss Simpson ballet and tap. They all claimed godparent status, so we had to be really creative to get away with what we got away with.

But the summer Belinda and I turned fifteen, the Rosenwald began to self-destruct, destroying her along with it. Prosperity moved out, and her illegitimate child, poverty, moved in. Residents who could afford it packed their three-bedroom, two car garage and white picket-fenced dreams, and bought houses on the other side of Chi-Town. The "no" people, who couldn't afford it, packed their anger and their frustration and moved into the Rosenwald. The once open spaces where flowers grew and fish swam and birds sang became crowded, trampled, smothered by the too-many-children-for-a-two-bedroom-apartment people.

Too many people's people. The kids who lived next door to me were the half-brothers and sisters of the kids who lived one floor under Belinda, and even some of them had kids of their own. Their daddy lived with another woman who had another half-brother or sister on the way. And all the kids were as angry as their parents. At first we tried. Did they want to be friends? "No!" Were they going to the same school. "No!" We offered to buy, did they want to go to Walgreens for a root beer float or a cherry coke? "No!" The looks on their faces was always, "No!" so after awhile we quit asking. Their answers were always "No!" but they hated it, and us, when we responded the same. Especially the boys. I mean men. They hated to be called boys.

When the boy/men asked me if I would let them "Cop a feel," I said, "No!" When the cute boy/man asked Belinda if she would show him this place he'd heard about called the "Submarine" she thought about it for a while (because she was tempted, and always faster than I was) but finally said, "No!" A hunch made us say, "No!" when asked to go to the Met or the Regal, even if James Brown was the headliner. "No!" to walks around the roof, or down in the basement. Even Mr. Watchman's "Maybes!" to us, had become "No!" to them; he wheezed a little faster, guarded us a little closer. Precautions were taken: he jiggled the gates after he banged them shut at 10:00 p.m. But he was only locking in what he was trying to lock out, shutting the gate after the Trojan horse had already been rolled in.

Anger demands space. Possibly due to generosity, but more likely due to fear, 47th Street, and therefore the Rosenwald, strained to contain the overflow, stuttering, "Yes" when it should have said, "No!" There weren't shouted, but there were whispered "Nos!"

disguised as bars across store's front windows, "Going out of business"/"Closed for remodeling" (never to open again) signs, and new hours posted, 9:00 a.m. to 6:00 p.m., so owners could head home before dark. Because "Nos!" were met head up, stared down and forced to say "Yes" in the face of switch blades and guns.

Prosperity hadn't paid a visit to our apartment yet, but afterwards, my parents and I, like unexpected, grudgingly accepted poor relations, moved in with her on another side of Chi-Town. Belinda's mother moved into that silent place inside herself where madness and grief settled in for an extended visit; Belinda's father rented a stool at Smokey's Bar. But before it happened, and even though it hurt and I was too afraid to tell my parents, I gave in. Belinda held out a little too long.

I met him every day, where he told me to, on my way to school. He picked my curls into an 8" afro, pulled out my pearl posts and replaced them with huge gold-plated hoops, and called me by a name that sounded like Ali-Baba. When he backed me up against the wall of the "Submarine" and stuck his fingers in my panties His determination forced a "Yes." He mercurichromed my feelings by saying it wouldn't hurt so much the next time. It was 4:30 p.m. Mr. Watchman was off duty that day but the gates were still locked at 10:00 p.m.

Belinda (she always held her ground better than I did) refused. The public defender pleaded that the boy/man was the product of a "No!" home: he'd been told, "No!" by too many teachers, too many employers, by life in general. Belinda's "No!" as she walked out of the laundry room and headed for the stairway had been one too many. Remedials classes hadn't been government funded then so the man couldn't take an education; affirmative actions hadn't been passed yet so he couldn't take a job. But with a switchblade in his hand he could take Belinda and did. The scratch marks on his face proved Belinda had yelled, "No" before she was silenced forever. Mr. Watchman was probably on the roof at the time, he didn't usually patrol the basement until later in the evening.

At Belinda's death, the Rosenwald exploded, 47th Street deteriorated.

DAVIDA KILGORE writes of herself and her writing:

"I was born May 9, 1956 in Chicago, attended Howalton Day School and Francis W. Packer High School. Later, I moved to St. Paul, Minnesota to attend Macalester College and the University of Minnesota. I became a single parent in 1976.

"I knew from the age of eight that I would eventually become an artist: writer, painter, musician, actor . . . any field where I could share my passions with others. Since I was an only child, my parents could afford to indulge my interests and so I attended the Art Institute of Chicago in the summers, had a drawing published in a book of children's poetry, joined 'Say' Children's Theatre, and took years of piano lessons.

"I was read to a lot when I was a child by my mother and others – *The Wizard of Oz*, *Bible Stories for Young Children* and *The Hobbit*. I went to sleep dreaming – my way of praying in those days – of the power to use words. Soon, I started to write. And I read everything I could get my hands on. I still believe that is the best way to learn to write – to absorb as many words as possible.

"Because I write for the same reason I breathe, eat, sleep, make love, form friendships and relationships . . . dare to begin new ones, sometimes speak when I should listen, sometimes retreat when I should attack, mother, care-take, like and love – that's just the way I am. Words and I belong to each other, we're monogamous lovers, maintaining loyalty to each other, even when my characters won't do what I tell them to do and usually win the battle. When I'm depressed, they're there waiting to cheer me up. When I'm happy, they jump on to the page faster than I can write them. When I procrastinate because of my busy schedule, they demand equal time by chasing me, finding me through overheard conversations in grocery check-out lines, confidences shared on crowded buses by complete strangers, crying guests on talk-shows struggling to express the same emotions I'm writing about in a story or a novel.

"I write for me. And if somewhere along the line my writing helps one other person, makes her laugh or cry or get angry, then I've succeeded. And although a steady job would help the lights stay on, keep the freezer stocked and the closets filled with the up-to-the-latest, it just can't beat the satisfaction of typing 'The End' at the bottom of a finished page."